A King Production presents…

Trife Life To Lavish

Part 3

Family Blood Ties

A Novel

JOY DEJA KING

ISBN 13: 978-1-958834-58-9
ISBN 10: 1-958834-58-0
Cover concept by Joy Deja King
Cover Model: Joy Deja King

Library of Congress Cataloging-in-Publication Data;
King, Deja Joy
Trife Life To Lavish Part 3: a novel/by Joy Deja King
For complete Library of Congress Copyright info visit;
www.joydejaking.com Twitter: @joydejaking

A King Production
P.O. Box 912, Collierville, TN 38027
A King Production and the above portrayal log are trademarks
of A King Production LLC

This Book is Dedicated To My:

Family, Readers and Supporters.
I LOVE you guys so much. Please believe that!!

~ Joy Deja King ~

"Each Betrayal Begins With Trust
Blood Makes You Related
Loyalty Makes You Family..."

A KING PRODUCTION
Trife Life
To
Lavish
Part 3
Family Blood Ties
JOY DEJA KING

Pretty Lies

Chapter One

The fluorescent light above her flickered like it had a vendetta. The bathroom stall reeked of bleach and panic. Pilar sat on the toilet lid inside the women's restroom at a Greyhound station in Baton Rouge. Her heels were off. Her stockings were torn. Her hands—trembling, slick with sweat—were streaked with something that might've been blood. She couldn't even remember how it got there.

The terminal was still except for the low hum of vending machines and the occasional crackle of the intercom. Pilar clutched the burner phone in her lap like it was a life raft. One bar of signal. That was it. In her possession: a single duffel bag stuffed with scattered cash, a passport she wasn't sure was real, and a heart pounding so hard it made her ears ring. She leaned her head back against the cold tile. Sharp reality. No illusions.

"I should've never taken that first check."

Everything had started so simple. One text. One job interview. One drink. Then came the late-night calls. The apartment with the skyline view. The designer heels and private dinners. And then... the trip.

Renny O'Neal. And his wife Genevieve. Together, they were supposed to be untouchable. And for a minute, Pilar thought she could be too. But this wasn't luxury. This was a cage—wrapped in silk, disguised with champagne, lined with secrets.

"Final call for Houston departure, platform six," the intercom echoed through the restroom. Her head snapped up. That was her bus. She shoved the burner phone into her bag, yanked on her heels without buckling them, and pushed out of the stall. Her reflection in the mirror made her flinch. Mascara smudged. Eyes hollow. She looked like a woman who had seen too much and survived just enough. And she wasn't done running.

"Not yet," she whispered. "You don't break until you're out."

She paused at the edge of the hallway. Going back to Houston was the last thing she wanted. But she didn't have a choice. Not after what she'd left behind. This wasn't about Renny. Or Genevieve. This was about survival. And if she didn't finish what she started... she might never make it out alive.

Pilar sprinted toward platform six, clutching her bag. As she climbed onto the bus, she felt eyes on her—an older man in a worn denim jacket, a teenage girl chewing gum too hard—but no one looked like they recognized her. Still, she kept her head down. Just in case. Because if her enemies figured out where she was headed... it wouldn't matter what bus she caught.

The Greyhound jolted over a pothole on I-10, and Pilar woke up with a gasp. She was sweating. Her neck ached. She didn't even know what time it was. She reached for her phone—then remembered it was off. Burner only now.

In her bag was a small notebook, the one Genevieve had given her during that first "training" week. Inside were names, addresses, amounts. Pilar didn't know if any of it was real or just planted to test her. But she'd memorized every line. Just in case. Because deep down, she'd always known this life had an expiration date. That the glamor was temporary. That the price was survival.

And now? It was time to pay.

Three Months Earlier...

The sunlight poured in through the glass-paneled doors of a second-floor master suite in the River Oaks district of Houston, Texas. The bedroom was the kind of luxury that whispered wealth, not screamed it—Egyptian cotton sheets, imported Italian marble, a walk-in closet the size of a one-bedroom apartment in Queens.

Genevieve O'Neal stood barefoot in front of a custom backlit vanity mirror; silk robe draped across her shoulders like it belonged to royalty. Her hair was styled in a soft, elegant chignon. Her nails were the color of vintage wine. Diamond studs winked at her ears. She looked expensive because she was. Not because of her husband. She'd rebuilt her life brick by brick—after every betrayal, every lie, every memory that once threatened to swallow her whole.

Now, applying her lipstick—Chanel, deep berry—Genevieve locked eyes with her reflection.

"Nichelle was a survivor," she said aloud, smoothing the corner of her mouth with slow precision. "But Genevieve? Genevieve is a brand I created."

She didn't say it for applause. It wasn't a mantra or affirmation. It was fact.

The girl from Queens who cried over Carmelo? Dead and buried.

The woman who torched Renny's favorite foreign whip after finding out he orchestrated Carmelo's death? Reborn.

Now she was Genevieve O'Neal. Wife of Renny—Renaldo O'Neal. CEO. Strategist. Curator of luxury. And most importantly, a woman who never let emotions write the terms of her life again. Her phone chimed:

Reminder: Walk-through at The Lounge. VIP suite inspection before press preview. Noon.

Genevieve walked across the bedroom and stepped into the dressing room, sliding open the wardrobe doors. Her fingers brushed past designer labels until she landed on a soft cream two-piece set from Hanifa, paired with minimalist gold heels. The look said: refined, powerful, unforgettable. Just the way she liked it. She pulled her robe off and stepped into her new skin for the day.

By noon, Genevieve stood inside her members-only lounge, The Garden Room—Houston's most exclusive hidden jewel. From the outside, it looked like a restored art gallery: whitewashed walls, black ironwork, no signage. Inside, it was a different world—floor-to-ceiling glass, velvet booths, hand-poured terrazzo floors, ambient lighting, and music that pulsed low, just loud enough to soundtrack million-dollar whispers.

Genevieve moved through the space slowly, heels clicking soft on marble. She passed her general manager, Kourtni—a slim woman with sharp eyes—who was locking in final details for that night's wine tasting.

"Press table's set. Chef's reviewing final pairings now," Kourtni reported.

Genevieve nodded. "Good. Make sure security's tight tonight. Nobody gets past the curtain unless they're on my list."

"Of course."

Inside the VIP suite—private bar, custom art, black satin drapes—Genevieve's phone buzzed.

A text from Renny:

Heading out now. Meeting might run long. Won't make dinner. Love you. —R.

She stared at the message. *Love you.* So simple. So hollow. She knew Renny was working something behind the scenes—something criminal he thought she didn't know about. So, she said nothing. Not yet. Because silence, when wielded right, was more powerful than confrontation.

Especially when you owned the room.

Welcome To The Garden

Chapter Two

Genevieve's phone lit up on the marble night-stand beside her espresso cup, the name ***Genesis*** glowing across the screen. She grabbed it quickly, standing by the floor-to-ceiling windows in her private study overlooking the lush, trimmed grounds of the O'Neal estate.

"Big brother!" she said excitedly. "I was just thinking about you."

"I'm always thinking about my baby sister. I apologize it took me a couple days to return your call. You good? I figured if you weren't, you would've sent me a 911 text," Genesis replied. His voice was deep, clipped, familiar—and just a little too calm.

Genevieve smiled, pacing slowly. "Yes. I'm good. I wanted to come see y'all. Thought I'd bring Elijah before he leaves for summer vacation with his best friend's family. School's out soon, and I haven't seen your baby girl in a while. I need some quality time with my little namesake. And Amir's son Desi. I know they've both gotten so big. How's Talisa—Lord knows I miss her." Genevieve was rambling on before she realized Genesis was not responding.

There was a pause. Not long enough to ignore, but just long enough for her to feel it in her gut.

"Yeah," Genesis finally said. "That sounds good. But uh... might not be the best time right now. I got some things going on."

Her brow furrowed. "What kind of things?"

"Just some business I need to handle," he said carefully. "I sent Talisa and Genie away for a little while. Didn't want them around while I dealt with it."

Genevieve leaned against the window frame, sensing some hesitation. "You don't want to talk about it over the phone."

"Exactly."

She sighed. "You sure you're good?"

"I'm solid. Once everything settles, I want y'all to come up. Stay as long as you like."

"I'd like that."

"Me too."

They hung up shortly after, but the weight of the call lingered. Genevieve stared out across the grounds; her arms crossed tight over her robe. Something was off. She knew her brother. That voice? That quiet edge in his tone? It meant war was brewing., and he didn't want her anywhere near it.

Pilar was thirty minutes early. Not because she was trying to impress anyone—but because she hadn't slept all night. Her mind had been racing since that cryptic text from Renny's assistant: **Wear black. Be quiet. Come alone**.

She did exactly that. She stood outside a nondescript building in Houston's River Oaks district, surrounded by million-dollar homes and manicured hedges. The structure looked more like a private gallery than a business—no sign, no doorbell, just a tall, dark wood entrance and a keypad.

Pilar double-checked the address Renny had sent her. Then she took a breath, lifted her chin, and knocked. The door clicked open on its own. Inside was all shadow and gold. The lighting was low, casting soft glows across velvet seating, moody art, and polished marble floors. Music played—Sade, maybe—smooth and warm like honey. The air smelled like sandalwood and citrus. It was luxury. A woman approached from the left hallway—tall, caramel-toned, tailored black blazer, no smile. She didn't introduce herself.

"Follow me."

Pilar followed. Down the hallway. Past a locked room. Past another. Until they reached double doors at the end. The woman opened them without knocking. Genevieve O'Neal sat at the center of a round table, flipping through a folder. She didn't look up right away. Pilar stood still, clutching her purse like it might fly away if she loosened her grip.

When Genevieve finally looked up, her eyes were sharp and unreadable. Her voice was smooth as silk.

"You're early."

"Traffic was light," Pilar said softly.

Genevieve closed the folder and studied her. "It's bette r to be early than late," she smiled, sizing up her attire. "You wore the right thing. Good. Let me ask you something, Pilar... are you loyal?"

That caught her off guard.

"I... I think so."

Genevieve arched an eyebrow. "You think so, or you are?"

Pilar swallowed. "I am."

"We'll see."

She stood and walked around the table, circling Pilar once like she was studying a sculpture. "You're pretty. But pretty doesn't last. What does last is discretion. Timing, discipline and how to maneuver under pressure." She paused in front of her. "Do you understand what this place is?"

Pilar shook her head.

"This isn't a lounge," Genevieve said. "It's a filter. People walk in one way and leave another. Business happens here that can't happen anywhere else."

Pilar nodded, unsure if a response was required.

"Tonight," Genevieve continued, "you'll be hosting a private table. Don't speak unless spoken to. Don't drink. Don't ask questions. Smile, but only when you mean it. And if someone offers you anything—anything at all—you bring it to me first. Understood?"

"Yes."

Genevieve stared a second longer. Then she handed her a small velvet folder. Inside was a slim metal card—no name, just the engraved symbol of a rose.

"Welcome to The Garden Room."

Pilar held the card like it might burn through her fingers. She felt the shift instantly. This wasn't a waitress gig. This was a test. An audition. A door. And she felt a sense of thrill that she had stepped through it.

The Garden Room was buzzing on Pilar's first night—but not on some booty-cheeks-gotta-shake type vibe she was used to. This was high class. Money long. Private tables. Candlelight. Muted jazz in the background. Pillars of Houston society mingled with quiet killers in designer suits. Deals were struck behind velvet curtains. Everything looked elegant... but Pilar could feel the tension humming beneath it all.

She moved gracefully, sticking to her lane—refilling glasses, adjusting menus, smiling just enough. The table she was assigned to held two sharply dressed men and a woman with a voice like smoke and sarcasm.

They barely looked at her. But one of the men—a tall, bald figure with a scar slicing through his left eyebrow—kept eyeing her. Not in a sexual way, but with something heavier. It made her skin crawl.

She kept her head down. Professional. Polished. Just like Genevieve had trained her. But just as she turned to leave the table, she caught a word.

"Maverick."

He said it low, to the man beside him. Barely above a whisper. But that name struck Pilar like ice down her spine.

She hesitated—just for a second too long.

"Problem?" the woman asked, raising a perfectly plucked brow.

Pilar recovered. "No, ma'am. Just making sure everything is perfect." She flashed a quick smile and hurried off.

In the back hallway, she paused to steady her breathing. She knew that name from a girl she used to run with back in ATL. Maverick wasn't a common name—and if it was *that* Maverick, he was treacherous. The kind of man whispered about in rooms that people didn't walk out of. Bodies. Disappearances. A criminal enterprise wrapped in violence and silence.

Genevieve appeared beside her like smoke.

"Something or someone catch your attention?"

Pilar jumped.

"No," she lied quickly. "Nothing worth repeating."

Genevieve did a quick assessment. "Remember, you're not the only one watching. Don't ever stop listening—but be careful what you do with what you hear."

Pilar nodded; throat dry.

Genevieve leaned in closer, her voice a soft blade. "You're either useful in this world... or you're in the way. Which one do you want to be, Pilar?"

Pilar didn't answer. She didn't have to. The choice had already been made the second she walked through that door.

Smoke Signals

Chapter Three

The bass was thick enough to make the leather seats vibrate. Inside the VIP suite at Club Dynasty—Houston's most infamous after-dark playground—the air dripped with lavender body oil, spilled cognac, and unspoken rules. Red lights pulsed low and moody, shadows moving like they had secrets to keep and money to launder.

Renny O'Neal leaned back on the curved couch, cigar smoke curling slow around his wrist. Black silk shirt, buttons undone, diamond watch catching the glow as he raised his glass of D'usse.

On his left, a dancer named Joya moved in the air inches from his lap—slow, seductive waves, never touching. On his right sat Midas and Dre—his most trusted men, though Renny knew better than to trust anyone for too long.

"We got a problem," Midas muttered, eyes tracking the room as the music slid into something slower.

Renny didn't flinch. "Of course we do."

Dre chuckled. "That route we tested through Port Arthur? It ain't clean no more. Somebody hit it two nights ago."

Renny exhaled through his nose, swirling his drink. "Hit it how?"

"Clean. Quick. Like they knew exactly when and where to strike," Dre said. "Didn't even trip the scout."

"Which means they had eyes inside," Renny said.

Midas nodded. "Or ears."

Renny leaned forward slow, setting his glass on the edge of the table. The music thumped beneath them, but his voice cut straight through it.

"How much did we lose?"

Dre hesitated. "Almost a hundred K."

Renny didn't blink. "That's rent money. I ain't stressing the amount—I'm stressing the principle." He turned to Midas. "Who?"

Midas scratched his beard. "Couple whispers say a name been floating."

"I'm listening."

"Maverick."

Renny's brow lifted. "Genesis' Maverick?"

Midas nodded slow. "Could be. Word is he's been expanding. Pressuring smaller ports, buying up people we thought were neutral."

Renny sat back, jaw tight. "If that's true, that ain't no coincidence."

"You think he's aiming at us? Or Genesis?" Dre asked.

"What difference does it make?" Renny muttered. "The fire don't care who lit the match. We all get burned the same."

His phone buzzed. He glanced at it—Genevieve.

Met Pilar. She'll do. Started work today. Remind you of anyone?

Renny smirked and typed back:

If she reminds you of you, I feel sorry for her.

Then another message:

Be home late. Handle your business, but I'm here if you need me.

He slipped the phone back into his pocket,

gaze returning to his crew.

"Double up on the next run. And get eyes on that name. If it is Maverick, I wanna know what he's doing in Texas, and why he think he can breathe my air without checking in first."

Midas and Dre nodded, the weight of the moment settling in.

Renny leaned back as Joya slid down the pole like honey. He looked calm. But in his mind? Smoke was already turning into fire. And if Maverick wanted heat? Houston had plenty to give.

An hour later, Renny exited through the private entrance of Club Dynasty. His driver opened the door of the matte black Escalade, and he slid in without a word. The moment the door closed; the illusion of the club faded.

"What do we know about the scout who missed the drop?" he asked without looking up.

"Name's D-Lo. Been solid so far," Midas said, riding shotgun. "But it's his cousin who put him on. That cousin just got out the feds."

Renny sucked his teeth. "And we didn't vet that?"

Dre shifted in the back seat. "He came up clean. No direct heat. But you know how them quiet types move. They never show you everything."

"Find him," Renny said. "Sit him down. Not hard, not soft. Just enough pressure to see if he cracks."

He glanced out the window. The city blurred past in red and gold.

"And if he do crack," Midas asked. "Then what?"

Renny didn't hesitate. "Then we sweep every inch of the tree. Cut off the branches. Burn the roots."

The SUV rolled on in silence. Outside, the streets looked calm. But under the surface, pressure was building. And Renny knew better than anyone—smoke always meant fire was coming.

Far away in the quiet back office of a private estate in upstate New York, Maverick stood over a digital map displayed on a massive screen. His silhouette stretched across the polished wood floor, backlit by low amber lighting. Cortez Mercer, the man who had been at The Garden Room—slim, suited, face scarred just enough to suggest survival—stood across from him, arms folded.

"You were right," Cortez said. "She's, his sister. Genevieve O'Neal. Runs the Garden Room in Houston. Married to Renny O'Neal."

Maverick cracked a faint smile. "Perfect."

"I didn't raise any suspicions, and no one recognized me."

"Of course not," Maverick said, circling the room slowly. "That's why I sent *you*. You blend. They never see you until it's too late."

He stopped in front of a tray holding two glasses and a bottle of aged scotch. He poured himself a glass but didn't drink it. "Keep going," he said.

Cortez nodded. "The club is clean. But people talk. Her new hire, a girl named Pilar? She's hungry. Still green. I saw the way she watched us. She's the type that needs purpose. Direction."

Maverick turned, eyes narrowing.

"Then give it to her."

Cortez blinked. "You want her turned?"

"I want her used. Whether she knows it or not." Maverick stepped closer to the screen, tapped the digital map to zoom in on Houston. "We don't take Genesis down through the front door. We hit the corners. We disrupt the rhythm. Make the people he loves move different. Mistrust each other. Second-guess themselves." He turned back to his business partner and ally.

"Genevieve is leverage. Renny is noise. But that girl?" he smiled now, cold and quiet. "That girl might be the thread that unravels the whole muthafuckin' sweater."

Quiet Moves

Chapter Four

Genevieve sat on the edge of her Le Marais chaise, walnut and gold leaf gleaming under the morning sun. She dusted a hint of highlighter across her cheekbone, the kind that made light bend just right in a room full of power. Her reflection in the antique vanity mirror looked calm, in control. But inside? Her mind was spinning.

Behind her, Renny leaned in the closet doorway, shirtless, steam still clinging to him from the shower, towel slung low. He was watching her, the same way he always did—half protection, half possession.

"You really think she ready?" he asked, tone neutral.

Genevieve gave a slow smile. "Pilar? She's raw. But she listens and learns quick. That matters. And she ain't scared of the room."

"You not worried she gon' fold when it get tight?"

Genevieve turned just enough to catch his gaze. "No more than I was with any of the others. But this one? She different. Got a quiet fight in her. Like somebody who's been takin' notes her whole life. Just needed the right opportunity."

Renny nodded. "Where you find her again?"

"Technically, she found me," Genevieve replied. "But that's a silly question—especially since you're the one who sent her my way, right?"

He grinned. "True. But I didn't know it was that obvious."

"It was," she said with a teasing laugh. "Now, tell me. How exactly do you know her?"

"She came up in a crew we used to do light work with. Said she was tired of door money and VIP scraps. Told me she had range. She was young but hungry. I gave her a number and told her—if she made it to Houston, I'd see what she was about."

Genevieve turned back to the mirror, applying a soft matte lipstick. "Well, she made it. And she's already catching attention."

Renny stepped into the bedroom, his towel replaced with fitted slacks now, watch already strapped on. "Well. make sure she don't drown," he said, leaning down to kiss Genevieve's shoulder. "'Cause these sharks out here? They don't nibble. They eat whole."

Genevieve held his eyes in the mirror. "If she drowns, it won't be from the deep water. It'll be because somebody dragged her under. But I'll make sure they never surface again."

He smirked, brushing a curl off her temple. "That's why I married you."

"No, you married me because I don't break."

Renny walked over and kissed his wife's shoulder. "You like her," he said it more as a statement than question.

"I do, but of course I don't trust her yet," Genevieve replied. "However, I do see potential, and I respect her hustle."

Renny grinned. "That's why I sent her your way. I knew you'd take to her."

Genevieve rolled her eyes playfully, then paused. Her tone softened. "I called Genesis yesterday."

Renny's smile faded just slightly. "Yeah?"

"I wanted to visit. Bring Elijah before he leaves with his friend's family for the summer. I miss the kids. I haven't seen little Genevieve since she first started walking. And Amir's boy... I just want to lay eyes on him again. I only saw him briefly when I stopped through Miami a few months ago. I feel this need to make sure everyone is okay."

Renny sat on the edge of the bed. "What did Genesis say?"

"Told me he's handling business. Sent Talisa and Genie away to make sure they stay safe. But he didn't want to go into details over the phone. He insisted it's under control."

Renny nodded but said nothing. He didn't want to put any more stress on Genevieve. Not when he was still piecing together if the person trying to cause problems for his operations was the same man Genesis was having problems with.

"He say what kind of business?"

"Not really. Just that it was better we didn't visit until it blows over."

"You believe him?"

Genevieve gave a small shrug. "I believe he thinks he's got it under control. But that doesn't mean I'm not worried."

Renny stood and kissed her on the forehead. "He's been through worse. I remember when he went to war with Arnez. Your brother's made of steel."

Genevieve looked up at him. "Steel still bends under pressure. I just hope there's no need for him to be war ready."

Renny met her gaze and nodded slowly. "If something shifts, he'll let you know. Genesis don't half-ass when it comes to family."

Genevieve exhaled, smoothing the front of her blouse. "I know. Still, I hate feeling like something's bubbling under the surface."

Renny walked over, kissed her one more time on the cheek. "If it is, he'll handle it. And if he can't, we will."

That brought the faintest smile to her lips. Genevieve straightened her spine and slid on her heels, the boss version of herself snapping back into place with practiced ease, as business was calling.

"Let's get to it," she said, grabbing her phone. "The Garden Room doesn't run itself," she remarked as they exited the bedroom to head downstairs.

Renny opened the door and gestured for her to lead. "After you, Mrs. O'Neal."

As they descended the stairs together, neither said what they were both thinking—that something was coming. They just didn't know what form it would take... yet.

Pilar stepped out of a black car and adjusted the hem of her dress. It was only noon, but she had a private client brunch scheduled at The Garden Room, and Genevieve had handpicked her to float between tables. She was nervous, but she'd never show it. Inside the lounge, everything was perfection. Pilar was focused, poised, alert—until a woman she didn't recognize brushed past her.

"Cute shoes," the woman said with a smirk. "Real leather?"

Pilar side eyed her. She was maybe mid-20s, honey skin, body wave bundles tucked under a designer headband. Her smile was warm, but there was something misleading behind it.

"I think," Pilar shrugged. "You work here?"

"Starting today. I'm Shay." She held out her hand, polished nails gleaming. "I heard you were the one to watch."

Pilar shook her hand cautiously. "Who told you that?"

"A mutual friend," Shay said. "Said if I wanted to make moves, I should get close to you."

Pilar smiled politely, "They lied." She didn't have friends in Houston. And she definitely didn't remember anyone mentioning a Shay.

Still, Shay didn't budge. "Come on. Show me the ropes. I'm a fast learner."

As they walked together into the belly of The Garden Room, Pilar felt the hair on her arms stand up. Something about Shay didn't feel right but she was an employee just like her. For all she knew, Genevieve was testing her. So, for now, Pilar smiled and kept walking.

Later that afternoon, Pilar caught Shay outside the staff locker room, leaning against the wall like she'd been waiting for her.

"You off?" Shay asked.

"Yeah. Why?"

Shay pulled a set of car keys from her pocket and twirled them on one finger. "I got a spot we can hit. Not far. Real chill. You look like you could use a drink."

Pilar hesitated. She was tired. And she didn't trust this girl. But she also knew better than to come off cold.

"Sure. One drink."

They drove in Shay's car—a sleek, jet-black two-door coupe with tinted windows and a low purr. Expensive but quiet. Like its owner. The bar was inside an upscale hotel in Midtown, dimly lit with plush seating and a low jazz playlist humming through the speakers. Pilar kept her guard up, sipping slowly, letting Shay do the talking.

Shay was charming. Smart. Said she used to model in Miami, worked promotions, did some light marketing. But she dropped breadcrumbs about wanting something more—something with real power, real money.

"You ever feel like you're meant for bigger?" Shay asked suddenly.

Pilar stopped mid sip. "What do you mean?"

"Like you're stuck in the audition phase, and you're just waiting for somebody to realize you've been the main character the whole time."

Pilar stared at her for a long moment. "Yeah," she said finally. "All the time."

Shay smiled like she'd just confirmed something. "Good," she said. "Then we're gonna get along just fine."

Just then, two well-dressed men entered the lounge, heading in their direction. One of them locked eyes with Shay and smiled. He was tall, caramel-toned, with low waves and a diamond link bracelet that cost a grip. The other man was the same height with chocolate skin, even white teeth and a smooth bald head.

"Ladies," he greeted smoothly.

"Hey, Trent," Shay said casually, standing to kiss him on the cheek. "Didn't expect to see you tonight."

"I was in the area," he said, sliding into the booth beside Shay. His friend sat next to Pilar, giving her a polite nod. "Who's your girl?"

"Trent, this is Pilar."

"Pleasure," he said.

Pilar shook his hand and offered a reserved smile. "Nice to meet you."

"And I'm Brice," the chocolate cutie said. His presence was confident, easy. He didn't try too hard. They made small talk about music, if she enjoyed working at The Garden Room, and favorite travel spots. Pilar found herself laughing more than she expected.

Brice had charisma. A charm that wasn't overbearing. And he looked at her like he saw something past the surface. Which was exactly what Shay had intended. As the conversation flowed, Shay sat back and sipped her drink, watching it all unfold. This was step one. Pilar had no idea she was already in the middle of a play.

The Garden Room was a different kind of beautiful at night. The air changed—heavier with secrets, sweeter with ambition. Pilar stood behind the bar in the Champagne Lounge, dressed in a black silk halter and wide-leg pants that accentuated her toned curvy body. She looked and moved like money as if she'd been born in it, even if her roots were miles from luxury.

This was her first night solo. No Shay. No backup. Just her and the city's elite, filtering in like wolves in cashmere.

She poured Cristal into flutes without spilling a drop, recited tasting notes from memory, and kept her eyes open. Always. Every face was a clue. Every compliment could be a mask.

"You're good," a voice said from the far end of the bar.

Pilar turned. Brice. Leaning back on a velvet stool like he owned the place. His black hoodie was designer—Balenciaga, probably—and his chains were tucked, but his watch was loud enough to speak for him. So were his eyes. They still had that undeniable chemistry.

"I'm working," she remarked, surprised to see him again so soon.

Brice grinned. "So am I."

She set down the bottle and leaned in just enough. "Shouldn't you be somewhere else? Doing whatever it is you do?"

"Maybe," he replied, eyes trailing the curve of her neck. "But this is the only place I want to be tonight."

She tried not to smile. Failed a little.

"You here to cause trouble?" she asked.

"I'm here to see you."

There was a pause. One of those thick, unspoken moments where the air seemed to pull tighter around them. Pilar swallowed it down and moved to the other end of the bar.

Brice didn't follow—didn't need to. His presence lingered like cologne.

An hour passed. The lounge buzzed with quiet laughter and the clink of crystal. Pilar did her rounds, made her tips, but she kept looking over. Brice stayed posted, nursing a neat pour of bourbon, eyes on her like she was the main act.

At midnight, he stood and dropped a tip so thick it could've paid off her phone bill and rent.

"See you soon," he said.

Pilar didn't answer. But her eyes did.

Chapter Five

The luxury condo overlooking downtown Houston was the kind of place you didn't find on real estate sites. Private elevator access, bulletproof windows, biometric locks. The kind of place that whispered importance.

Inside, Shay sat across from Cortez. He poured two fingers of dark rum into a glass but didn't offer her any. Instead, he watched her the way a handler watches his most dangerous weapon.

"She likes me," Shay said, slipping off her coat

and draping it over the back of a leather chair. "Still guarded, but curious. She took the bait."

"How deep?" Cortez asked.

"She agreed to drinks. Talked a little about her past. Not much. But enough. She doesn't easily trust people. That works in our favor."

He nodded, swirling the rum in his glass. "And the man?"

"Trent showed up with a man named Brice. Just like you said. What you didn't tell me, was that he was gonna be such a fine chocolate cutie," Shay commented getting no reaction from Cortez. "But they clicked. He didn't press too hard. He let her lean in. She responded."

Cortez smirked faintly. "Keep it subtle. We don't want her running. We want her to keep leaning. Just enough to reach for the rope we'll wrap around her neck later."

Shay tilted her head, studying him. "What's the endgame? You want her to spy on Genevieve?"

"No," he said. "We want her to be a distraction, so Genevieve doesn't see what's coming. If we do it right, Pilar won't even realize she's playing for the other side until she's already delivered what we need."

"And what's that?"

"Access. Disruption. Weak spots. Genevieve

has built a mini empire. But empires don't fall from the outside—they crumble from within."

He stood, walked over to the floor-to-ceiling window, and looked out across the city.

"Genesis thinks he's untouchable. If we can't get to him, we'll take down everyone that he loves until he is the last one standing. When his sister's life starts folding in on itself, let's see how long he'll stay in hiding. He'll have no choice but to show his face."

Shay said nothing, but her eyes gleamed with mischief and danger.

In the outskirts of the city, inside a soundproofed garage beneath a mechanic shop Renny used for quiet business, Dre and Midas stood across from a sweating, nervous D-Lo.

D-Lo was young, slim, cut but slightly goofy. Had the kind of energy that worked well in street-level work but made him terrible at hiding fear. Right now, fear rolled off him like heat.

"I told you, I ain't know nothing," D-Lo said for the third time, shifting in his seat.

Dre leaned against a metal table with his

arms folded, while Midas stood nearby in silence, with his jaw tight.

"You were the scout," Dre said. "That route was your responsibility. And we got hit. Somebody knew the timing, the itinerary, the drop spot. That ain't random."

"I ain't tell nobody!" D-Lo snapped. "I checked the spot twice before I gave the go-ahead. It was clean!"

"Until it wasn't," Midas said, his voice low and steady. "So, either you lying, or somebody you talk to ain't who they say they are."

D-Lo shook his head. "I don't be talkin' to nobody. I stay in my lane."

Dre walked over and pulled up a folding chair, spinning it backward and sitting across from D-Lo.

"What about your cousin?" Dre asked. "The one who just got out the feds. You staying with him, right?"

D-Lo's eyes shifted.

Midas caught it. "Uh huh. You paused. That's what we needed to see."

"He don't know nothin'," D-Lo muttered. "He ain't even in the loop."

"We haven't established that yet," Dre said, "you sure you wanna go out on the line and vouch for your cousin? Because somebody flipped that route, and it wasn't no guesswork. You been sol-id, D-Lo. But right now, your rep don't mean shit if product keeps disappearing."

Midas walked over to the wall and flipped open a small steel cabinet. Inside was a towel, gloves, and a heavy pipe wrapped in leather at the handle.

D-Lo flinched. "Yo, come on, man... I ain't no snitch, but I ain't no mole either."

Dre stayed seated, calm. "Then tell us who been around. Who's been asking questions. Who your cousin talking to. Who's paying attention even though they shouldn't be."

"He did have some dudes over last week," D-Lo admitted quickly. "Said they was from outta town but relocated to Houston. Supposed to be here for a few months. Get their business going. Big money types. One of 'em had a black Benz, New York plates."

Midas raised an eyebrow. "You just remem-bered that shit?"

"He ain't tell me they was into street shit. Said they was just talkin' real estate, tryna make legit moves."

"Did you get any names?" Dre asked.

D-Lo hesitated. "I heard one of 'em say

something like...Cort, Courtney...Something like that. Wait, nah it was Cortez. That's what it was," he nodded like he knew he finally got the name correct.

Dre and Midas exchanged a look.

"Cortez," Midas said under his breath.

Dre stood up. "Alright. That's all we needed."

D-Lo looked between them. "So, I'm good?"

"You on ice," Dre said. "Keep your head down. Tell your cousin the next time out-of-town money shows up at your door, you better check credentials before somebody checks him."

Midas added, "If you breathe wrong, we'll know. Don't make us come back."

They left D-Lo sweating in the chair, the heavy door clanging shut behind them. Once upstairs, Dre lit a cigarette as he walked out into the alley behind the shop. The Houston heat clung to his skin.

"You believe him?" Midas asked.

"Enough to know we not the only ones getting played," Dre said. "Somebody's using street kids like chess pieces. This Cortez nigga seems to be the one holding the board. But who the fuck is he."

Midas exhaled sharply. "He might be one of Maverick's men or he might be on the come up, making his own moves, regardless, Renny gonna want blood for this."

"He gon' get it," Dre said. "Soon as we find the hand behind the trigger."

Pilar sat on the edge of her bed, scrolling through her phone before she took it in for the night, when she saw a text from Brice.

Am I only gonna see you if I pop up at your job? Let me take you out.

She smiled. It felt nice to get some attention from a man she found attractive. Pilar didn't realize how lonely she was being in Houston by herself. But she also couldn't shake the slight chill she had the other night when she caught Shay watching her while immersed in her conversation with Brice. There was something about Shay that didn't line up. Too polished. Too perfect.

Still, her attraction to Brice made her ignore the doubts she had and replied to his text.

If that's what you want, make it happen.

She set the phone down and stared at the ceiling. Pilar had no idea how deep she was already in.

Slippery Ground

Chapter Six

Genevieve gazed out from her upstairs window, sipping her green juice while scrolling through her messages. The morning light bathed Houston in a golden hue, but her mood didn't reflect the beauty outside. She had a meeting lined up with the interior designer for the new expansion of The Garden Room, a project that should have filled her with excitement. However, the remark from Kourtni, her general manager the other day, gave her a sense of foreboding that she couldn't shake.

Pilar was slated to oversee operations between both lounges, a task that required finesse and attention to detail. Genevieve was confident she was ready. Shay had expressed a desire to shadow her, eager to learn the ropes. On paper, they seemed to be a perfect fit. Everything went seamlessly, except for an observation from Kourtni, that had her instincts screaming.

"Shay's a quick learner," she remarked, a warning edge to his voice. "But she doesn't just watch the guests. She watches the staff. She watches everything. Even you."

Genevieve had masked any outward concern, maintaining her poised demeanor. Yet, those words clung to her thoughts. Watching everything. Why Shay would be watching everything lingered in her mind. She wanted to believe that maybe Kourtni had gotten the wrong read while clocking the new hire, but if she was correct, she'd have to eliminate any potential threats.

This realization prompted her to instruct security to conduct thorough background checks on all personnel once more, with a particular focus on recent hires. Because in Genevieve's world, loyalty wasn't merely preferred—it was a crucial element for survival.

Pilar stepped into the lounge of a rooftop bar in Montrose. Brice was already there, nursing a drink and dressed in a crisp white button down and designer jeans. His smile was welcoming when he saw her.

"There she is," he said, standing to kiss her cheek.

Pilar smiled. "Were you early or am I just late?"

"I am early for certain people."

They sat, ordered drinks. The rooftop was quiet, intimate. Pilar felt herself relax. Working at The Garden Room, she was surrounded by upscale opulence, but it was also insanely intense. To the point, Pilar never had a moment to let down her guard. She needed to be on top of her game at all times, no slipping. Not only that, for once, someone wasn't trying to scam her or pitch a hustle, or so she thought. Brice asked questions. Real ones. Where she was from. What made her leave. Who she used to be before Houston. And his laidback approach made her want to answer. Not everything. But enough to feel that she was developing a genuine bond with someone.

A few tables away, Shay was nestled in a dimly lit corner, at the edge of the rooftop bar, wearing oversized sunglasses despite the waning sun. Her phone lay face-up next to a flute of champagne. With practiced nonchalance, she scrolled through her messages, feigning disinterest while keeping a close surveillance on Pilar and Brice. Cortez would appreciate her discretion, he always did. He would also be pleased with Brice. The way Pilar was smiling, being flirty and affectionate, his charisma had her leaning all the way in.

Midas stood in the surveillance room at The Garden Room, watching footage on the center screen, just as Renny demanded. He figured it would be a waste of time, but following his bosses' orders paid off.

"Yo, Dre," he called out. "You need to see this."

Dre stepped in, holding a coffee. "What's up?"

Midas pointed at the feed. "That's Shay. Look who she talking to by the loading dock last night."

Dre squinted. The camera caught Shay laughing with a man in a black hoodie. He handed her something small—maybe a phone, but he wasn't sure, then he walked off toward a silver coupe.

Midas froze the frame. "Renny told me to run the plate of any unfamiliar cars lurking in the vicinity. This car was here the other day, so I ran that plate. It's registered under a shell corp. One of the names tied to a New York LLC address."

"And the guy?" Dre asked.

"He's on this video talking to Shay but Pilar was with him last night at the rooftop spot in Montrose. Our people flagged it off Pilar's GPS. Renny wanted to keep eyes on her. They were having drinks."

Dre cursed under his breath. "So, wait, this nigga meeting for drinks with Pilar, while Shay having a mystery meeting with him by the loading dock?"

"Exactly."

Dre rubbed the back of his neck. "Maybe he tryna date both of them. This shit ain't making no sense."

"We have to take this to Renny. He'll get to the bottom of it. But he needs to know about this, and the name D-Lo provided us, Cortez. Immediately," Midas insisted.

When Shay pulled up to her complex, she called Cortez from the parking garage below her condo. Her voice echoed slightly in the enclosed space.

"Our girl is getting comfortable," Shay said. "Brice got her running that mouth like he, her therapist."

"What did she say?" Cortez wanted to know.

"Family situation. Strained. Mom in and out of her life. She's here alone. Trying to prove herself."

"Perfect, mean she's vulnerable." Cortez said, pleased with the update. "She'll cling to anyone who makes her feel important, that she matters. Brice can easily do that."

"Genevieve's watching her close though," Shay warned. "She's developed a soft spot for her."

"Let her. That means she's distracted. Distracted people miss the cracks forming beneath them. I'll be in touch," he hung up without saying another word to Shay.

Cortez paused briefly to contemplate his next move while standing in the back room of a high-end car dealership, which was actually a cover for one of the laundering operations he and Maverick ran. He then addressed a member of the regional team.

"Accelerate our Houston timeline," he said. "We move on the ports within two weeks. Genesis is already stretched. I want Renny under fire before he knows what hit him."

The man nodded. "And his wife?"

"Let her keep walking the edge. When she falls, she'll drag half their empire with her."

Later that night, Dre and Midas met with Renny back at the shop behind closed doors. The energy was tight. Controlled.

"It's a dude named Cortez," Dre said. "We got confirmation. D-Lo heard the name from one of his cousin's guests. NY plates. Quiet hitters. Supposedly they here, venturing into real estate. And Cortez might be actually living in Houston."

Renny leaned back, jaw tight. "I know that name."

"I did some digging. He's not associated with any underground sets. He move smooth. Gotta scar. Always wears suits like he don't touch dirt," Midas added.

"That's him," Renny nodded. He stood, walked to the edge of the room. Lit a cigar. "I'm willing to bet he one of Maverick's men. Here's what we do. Lock down all Garden Room vendor relationships. Cross-check staff. No new names slip through unless they've been fully vetted."

"They already might be in the building?" Dre sighed.

"What the fuck you mean?" Renny growled.

"I can't confirm if he works for Maverick, but a nigga named Brice has been communicating with both Pilar and Shay on what appears to be some personal shit. He got ties to New York and sniffing around two women that work at The Garden Room," Midas informed his boss.

"If they're coming for Genevieve, that makes it personal." Renny turned. Eyes cold now. "Find Cortez. Put eyes on Brice. And run background on anyone Pilar talks to more than once. If Shay blinks wrong, I wanna know what color her contacts are."

Dre nodded. "We on it."

Midas cracked his knuckles. "You want us to touch anybody yet?"

Renny shook his head. "Not yet. Let them

think we soft. Let them feel comfortable. Then when we hit back, they'll never see it coming."

Pilar was standing on her small balcony, sipping a glass of wine, thinking about Brice. He seemed to be occupying her thoughts whenever there was a quiet moment, like now. So, when her phone lit up with a text on the screen from him, she felt butterflies.

Next time I see you, I want to hear about your dreams. Maybe I can help make them come true.

She smiled while she typed back. ***Careful. I might force you to do that.***

Please do. Brice replied.

His response sent Pilar's mind into a whirlwind of thoughts. Her infatuation with Brice was intensifying. Not realizing she was being lead directly into a trap, as if she were a moth irresistibly drawn to a flame.

Love Bombing

Chapter Seven

Genevieve stood near the hostess podium, draped in a white silk jumpsuit that fit her like money. Tonight, The Garden Room was ablaze with energy, exuding a sultry aura, perfect for concealing the secrets of the wealthy and men with a dangerous allure. She monitored everything—each client, every shift in the room, and most importantly, kept a vigilant watch on Shay. Shay was stationed at her post, clipboard in hand, with a smile that was impeccably professional. It was all a bit too flawless, too polished.

Genevieve waved her over. "How are you feeling about working at The Garden Room?"

"Loving it," Shay said, without hesitation.

Genevieve nodded; eyes locked on her. "Are you watching Pilar closely?"

"Of course. I heard she's the one to learn from. I'm impressed with her work ethic. I can tell she's very driven."

"Yeah," Genevieve said, sipping her drink. "Drive can be dangerous when it's not pointed in the right direction."

Shay suddenly became silent which was rare. She kept her face calm, but Genevieve caught the flicker. That split-second flash in her eyes.

"I expect for you to be my eyes and ears, so inform me if you notice anything off," Genevieve instructed, then turned and walked away, intentionally leaving Shay unnerved. Her eyes widened as Genevieve vanished into the crowd, leaving her to wonder if she was being set up, but for what purpose? To test her loyalty to Genevieve, perhaps, and see if she'd snitch on her coworkers? Whatever the reason, Shay was determined to ensure she hadn't been compromised or exposed.

Pilar had the night off but still spent it at The Garden Room. She was two drinks in, lounging in one of the VIP suites, with Brice beside her. He was smooth, like her top-shelf wine—dressed in slacks, a printed linen sport shirt, and a diamond link bracelet that caught the light without screaming for attention. He wasn't flashy, he was calculated, as if he knew precisely how to slip past one's defenses and get under people's skin.

"You ever wanna own a spot like this?" Brice asked, leaning close.

Pilar scoffed. "You think they give girls like me keys to shit like this?"

Brice grinned. "They don't. You gotta take 'em."

"I like the way you said that. As if it could actually happen," she laughed," taking a sip of her wine.

"Because it can."

Pilar eyed Brice and then her heart began to race at the very idea of owning a place like The Garden Room. The power, the luxury, the control—it was all within reach, she just needed to seize it. But she was no Genevieve O'Neal, or could she be? Then a nagging voice in the back of her mind reminded her that nothing in this world came without a price. With Brice's words lingering in the air like a tantalizing promise, she couldn't help but wonder what his game truly was. Was he offering her a path to success, or leading her down a treacherous road of deceit and manipulation?

The music pulsing through the VIP suite, mixing with the clinking of glasses and low murmurs of conversation was disrupting Pilar's concerns regarding Brice's motives. Then she noticed Shay stealing a glance at her from across the room, her demeanor cool and collected, but there was something in those watchful eyes that put Pilar on edge. She couldn't shake the feeling that behind the facade of innocence lay a cunning mind and a dangerous agenda.

As the night progressed, and the effects of the alcohol began to take hold, the mood in The Garden Room shifted. Pilar found herself drawn into Brice's web, becoming intrigued and willing to surrender to her desires, as her inhibitions faded away. The temptation of power and luxury hovered enticingly near, whispering promises of a life she once thought unattainable, until Brice altered her reality.

Pilar had never experienced anything quite like this before. The warmth coursing through her body, the surge in her veins, and the persistent ache in her chest that remained after

Brice touched her as if he understood every facet of her soul. It wasn't just physical—it was psychological. Dangerous. Addictive.

Brice's gaze lingered on her with an intensity that felt like he branded her, his eyes reflecting a hunger, that transcended mere attraction. He exuded a predatory air, akin to a sleek, beautiful panther draped in designer attire. Despite every instinct warning her of engaging in such a risky game, the thrill was too intoxicating to resist. The sultry air of The Garden Room clung to her skin, yet it was the anticipation of what awaited ignited her senses. With a reckless abandon, Pilar disregarded all caution, her heart racing as she intertwined her fingers with Brice's. Together, they stepped into the cool night, the city bustling around them, lights dancing like temptation. Pilar didn't ask where they were going. She didn't care.

Brice led her to his apartment, it was everything she imagined: sleek, high-rise, glass walls, white marble floors, chrome accents, and a view that made her gasp. As the door closed with a click, Pilar found herself willingly trapped.

"I want you to become a part of my world," Brice said, voice silk over smoke. He tucked a strand of hair behind her ear, fingers grazing skin that melted at his touch. The lighting was low, golden, seductive. Their kiss was slow at first, then deeper. Intense. When he lifted her and carried her toward the bedroom, Pilar didn't resist. She welcomed the weightless feeling. Silk sheets. Soft moans. Skin on skin.

"Just relax," he murmured against her throat, every kiss like a drug. "Let me show you what it means to be wanted." And he did.

His tongue glided over her body as though charting a route for a seductive journey. She felt seen, devoured, and worshipped. His dick became a magical tool that hypnotized her pussy into submission. When they finally collapsed together, breathless, tangled in sheets and warmth, Pilar was undone. Spellbound. Owned.

The next week moved like a high—blurred edges, no brakes, just romance, sex, luxury on repeat and more sex. Pilar woke up to texts from Brice that felt like poetry dipped in game: voice notes laced in bass, a photo of his hand wrapped around a glass of dark liquor—skyline glowing behind it, that pinky ring gleaming like a threat.

By noon, a delivery boy would slide through The Garden Room with a fresh bouquet—tulips, orchids, roses and peonies wrapped in matte black paper, with the smell of temptation. Everything Brice did seemed effortless, like he was born knowing how to have you under his influence. No pressure, no strings. Just vibes, mystery, and gifts that said, *I got you,* even if she didn't know what he'd want in return.

He took her to this tucked-away French spot downtown—where the ambiance was dim lit, the waitstaff in denim-aprons, and a steak tartare garnished with a delicate quail egg. Pilar sat across from Brice, letting the candlelight stroke his cheekbones. He didn't just walk into a room— he shifted gravity. He played with language like it was foreplay, flipping between smooth talk and sharp wit with ease. Pilar let herself soak it in— his jokes, the way he always reached for the small of her back like she was already his.

By Wednesday, he had a black Escalade pull up to her place. Driver didn't say much except, "Miss, we're here." Rooftop restaurant, skyline glowing, river stretched out like a silver ribbon. Pilar stepped as if she owned the city—and for the first time, she almost believed it. Heads turned when they walked in. Hostess damn near bowed. And Brice? He acted as if it was just another day. Dinner hit different—three courses, no menus, Brice ordering for both of them like he read her cravings from her pulse. Dessert came with a jewelry box—matte black, velvet inside, gold chain with an anatomical diamond heart pendant. On the back, in tiny script, her name.

"Saw it. Thought of you," he said casually, making her believe dropping gifts was as routine as brushing his teeth.

Then came the spa days, shoes she once stared at behind glass now sitting in her closet, and a purse she didn't even know how to pronounce, dropped into her lap as they walked into some club where the walls pulsed like speakers. Pilar never said thank you out loud. She didn't need to. Her walk changed. Her look changed. Her world changed. She caught her reflection one night and paused—lip gloss on point, hair soft, collarbone kissed with shimmer, his scent still on her skin. She looked expensive, top-notch pedigree. As if the girl who counted change at the laundromat had been traded in for someone new.

Shay noticed. She watched like someone who knew how fairytales ended. Friday night, powder room, mirrors on every wall. Shay leaned into the counter, lip gloss in hand, but her tone came clipped.

"You glowing," Shay said, curious how Pilar would respond.

Pilar smirked. "Maybe I finally got some sleep."

Shay rolled her eyes. "Don't play me. What's his name?"

"Brice." Pilar said his name softer than she meant.

Shay paused, as if thinking. "Brice? Trent's Brice?" pretending not to know.

Pilar's brows pulled together. "Yes, that Brice."

"I didn't realize you all were seeing each other. It's been a minute; seems he has you open. But be careful. He got that look—like he can buy you, break you, and bounce before you catch your breath."

Pilar tried to laugh but it came out wrong. "He's not like that. He makes me feel..." She paused. "Special."

Shay shut her compact slow. "That's how it starts. Then one day you wake up and realize everything you are, is something *he* made."

"You jealous?" Pilar snapped.

Shay gave a sad smile. "Just seen too much.

With men like Brice, ain't nothing free. Not even love."

They exited the powder room together, yet the tension between them was heavy.

Pilar gave zero fucks about Shay's opinion of Brice. The next night, he took her to a gallery opening. She didn't know art, but the way he whispered stories about the paintings made each one a masterpiece. He held her hand close to his.

He didn't ask much. Didn't pry. Just studied her, responded to her. Touched her in ways that made her feel both adored and his personal possession.

The gifts kept coming. Tickets to a concert she didn't know was sold out. A silk scarf that made her skin glow. Perfume labeled *for your nights here.*

Pilar never felt him *ask* for anything. But somehow, she gave more of herself every day. Her outfits bent to his style. Her laugh echoed his rhythm. Every exit from his apartment felt like leaving a piece of herself behind. And the Garden Room noticed. She moved different. Collected tips like confessions. Guests remembered her name. Even the bartenders stopped being short.

But Shay stayed back. Watching. Studying. Like she was bracing for the fall. Yet, Pilar stayed floating. Untethered. Addicted to being in Brice's orbit. In her mind, she finally belonged. She didn't know it yet, but gravity was already pulling.

Chapter Eight

Genevieve's office was a study in controlled iciness. Black lacquered walls, smoked glass desk floating like a throne, and floor-to-ceiling windows showcasing Houston as if it was her kingdom. She stood in front of it, arms folded, posture steel straight.

Her assistant Sam, stepped in without a word, moving in silence not to disturb her thought process. He laid the black dossier dead center on the desk, no extra motion, no wasted energy. With one gloved finger, he flipped it open. Inside, receipts. Eight-by-ten surveillance shots in crisp color. First frame. Pilar stepping out of a black town car, hair slicked, posture like she knew she had eyes on her. Second? Her and Brice in some velvet-rope cocktail spot, his hand planted firm on the small of her back. She was looking up at him as if all the answers to her life were in his eyes. Third? Outside some bougie uptown boutique, his arm looped through hers, faces close like secrets were currency.

More photos; a sushi chef mid-slice. Pilar laughing and Brice leaning in, all presence and control. Not just attentive, possessive.

"Several different nights," the assistant said. Voice flat. "Gallery opening. Private club. Sushi spot in Midtown. They left together every time holding hands. One would think they were couple goals."

Genevieve scanned the images fast, like she was reading code buried in pixels. Sam slid out a smaller folder—navy, silver initials: S.W.

"Shay," he said. "We pulled school records, work history, socials. Looks clean. Too clean."

"Clean means wiped. Nobody's spotless in this city—not unless they paid for the bleach." Genevieve's voice hit like cold marble.

"She might be nothing," the assistant offered,

but his tone said he didn't believe it.

"She ain't nothing," Genevieve replied. "She's a cover story. And cover stories? Always got someone reading the script." She tapped her nail on the desk—three sharp knocks that echoed a warning. "Dig deeper. If she did attend college, start with her old roommate. And don't just scrape the surface. I want ghost data. The deleted shit."

The assistant nodded, thumbs already flying across his device. Genevieve pushed one photo toward the edge of the desk. It hovered, Pilar and Brice captured in the middle of a moment that didn't belong to either of them.

"And him," she continued. "Brice. Full run. Financials, court records, medical files. I want to know who he is, where he came from, and why he chose her. No one walks into my city clean. Not like this. Not at this level."

Sam straightened his tie. "There's one more thing," he said. "Cortez Mercer."

"The man my husband mentioned to me. I told you to look into him. You got some info?"

"We intercepted a call from someone in his crew. They're asking about Pilar. Low-key for now. Just feelers."

Genevieve's smile was cold, eyes still locked

on the photo.

"Everybody wants a piece of her all of a sudden, don't they," she murmured. "Wonder what they think makes her so special."

Sam cleared his throat, cautious. "Maybe she's bait."

Genevieve let the photo fall. It fluttered to the tile.

"I believe you are correct. But for now, let them think I'm asleep." She flicked her hand, dismissing him.

He left without another word. Door clicking shut behind him.

Genevieve turned back to the glass; the city's pulse reflected in her stare. Sirens, headlights, and tension stitched across the skyline like a heartbeat. Something was moving out there. A storm. She felt the tiniest prickle of fear beneath her skin. But Genevieve wasn't going to wait for it to hit.

Dre and Midas rolled up to an underground poker room run by Lex Bo, a soft-belly money man linked to Cortez Mercer. The spot was a basement joint two blocks from the river, hidden behind an abandoned storefront that sold TVs and empty boxes for cash. Word was the poker room held a cash reserve sizable enough to test the city's treasury, and every cent that changed hands in there got a cut taken by Cortez. The walls of the room sweated out a humid funk of cigar smoke, disinfectant, and plastic upholstery. The action never stopped: seven days, twenty-four hours, high stakes only, no randoms. Lex Bo liked to think that made him untouchable, but he was wrong.

Dre didn't waste time with the front. He and Midas circled the block twice, then cut through the alley, boot soles splashing through broken glass and puddles that smelled like spoiled gin. The back door was steel, but the frame was wood, and Dre's old army boot snapped it in half. Midas was right behind, mask up, hood tight, eyes cold and flat.

Inside, the table action froze mid-flush. Four players and two girls in halter tops all fixed on the hardware Dre had leveled at chest height: a black 9mm, gleaming like a fresh bruise in the fluorescent light. Nobody said a word. Midas swept his eyes over the chips, the bills, the flash of gold watch bands. Calculated the value of fear.

"Everybody out," Dre said, voice slow and deep as gunmetal. "Now!"

The air sucked out of the room. Players scrambled, chairs scraping, cash and chips abandoned in a panic as they bolted for the ruined door and vanished into the night. Only Lex Bo stayed seated, hands splayed on the cloth, fat face pulsing red with shock and the beginning of rage. He was a big man, but something in the way he stared at the muzzle said he'd seen this kind of thing go sideways before, and his bladder was not on his side.

Midas sauntered to the table, sweeping the stacks into a pile, then into a heap on the sticky linoleum. He flicked a lighter, watched the edges of the chips melt, the stench of burning plastic mingling with the fear Lex couldn't keep inside. Lex's lips trembled but he didn't dare speak. He looked at Dre, then at Midas, then at the chips, as if maybe it was all a test, and he just hadn't figured out the rules yet.

"That's your first warning," Dre said, his tone brutal but almost casual. "Next time, it's your blood on the floor. Not the paint."

Lex finally found his voice, or at least the ghost of it. "Cortez—Cortez said—"

Midas cut him off, dropping a prepaid burner phone next to the melting chips with a clatter that echoed off the cinderblock walls. "Cortez won't be taking your calls. You pick up when it rings, and you better pray you still matter when we do."

Lex stared at the phone, then up at the men. His hands were shaking now, sweat beading on his forehead and dripping onto the green cloth. He opened his mouth again, but Dre was already turning, mission done, message delivered. Midas paused at the threshold, gave Lex a look that was less a threat than a eulogy. They left the way they came through the shattered door, up the alley, vanishing into the night before sirens or second thoughts could catch up.

Lex sat there for a full minute, letting the heat and stink of the burning chips fill his lungs, the silent phone a new sun at the center of his universe. He pressed his hands together, knuckles white, and waited for the call that would decide whether he lived or died.

Execution Style

Chapter Nine

At a private strip on the outskirts of Houston, the wind cut hard across the tarmac like it had something to prove. Sodium lights buzzed above, painting the cracked runway in greasy gold. Cortez stood calm as ever in a camel trench, hands deep in his pockets, head tilted just enough to flex control without saying a word. The matte black jet behind him gleamed under the floodlights with secrets stashed in every panel. Fuel fumes and money hung thick in the air.

His crew moved like shadows in charcoal

jumpsuits, loading crate after crate into the plane's belly. No words, no fumbles. They knew better than to slip around Cortez. He kept the phone close to his ear even though nobody was within shouting distance. The static hit first, then Maverick's voice came through low, clipped, like he was already halfway through a plan.

"You sure it's time?" Maverick wanted confirmation.

Cortez gave it to him. "Lex is compromised. Renny's people already pressed him. Dumb fuck won't be able to keep his mouth shut. He spills anything—even by accident—and the ports, Galveston stash spots... gone."

There was a pause. The kind where you could almost hear Maverick thinking.

"So, he's dead weight," Maverick said. "Cut him."

Cortez nodded. "Diego's on it. Clean. No witnesses."

A loader tripped near the wheel well. Cortez clocked it but didn't move. One of his lieutenants corrected the man with a sharp smack to the head—no shouting, no scene. Tempo stayed perfect.

Maverick shifted the convo. "What about the girl?"

"Pilar's deep," Cortez said. "She's wrapped in Brice's grip. Shay's got eyes inside. It's lining up. We pull the trigger when the moment's right."

The corner of his mouth twitched like the ghost of a smile. Past the hangars, stars poked through the smog, and he thought about how every one of them could be a drop point, an escape route, or a kill zone. Depends on who drew the map. Wind kicked his coat open. A low hum from a nearby plane drowned out Maverick for a second. When the noise faded, the voice came back sharper.

"Don't get cocky, Cortez. Genevieve ain't one of these goofy bitches. Even though her brother is Genesis and her husband is Renny, she is self-made. One wrong scent and she'll torch the whole city to find you."

Cortez flicked his lighter open, flame dancing over his thumb before he snapped it shut.

"That's why we working her blind side. He ended the call, turned toward the hangar where Diego waited like a shadow come to life. Cortez lifted two fingers. Diego stepped forward.

"Lex Bo," Cortez said. "Make it quick. Make it quiet. Make it permanent."

Diego nodded. No words. Just pulled out a burner, dialed a number, and slipped into the dark.

Cortez lit a cigarette, letting the smoke curl around him like armor. The last crate slid into the hold. The pilot showed up at the bottom of the stairs, eyes forward, not too direct—smart. Every detail mattered. He pulled out a second phone, hit an encrypted line. One ring.

"Go."

"Lex is being handled. Strip is clean. Schedule's bumped twenty-four hours. Port team needs to prep for a new drop."

"Understood. Genevieve?"

Cortez exhaled slow. "Still looking the wrong way. Brice and Pilar are keeping her distracted."

He hung up. Engines roared as the jet prepped for takeoff.

Cortez stayed put, cigarette burning low, eyes locked on the horizon. Everything was in motion. And if anyone fell off the board? So be it. The game kept going.

Lex Bo sat in the poker room's back office, hands trembling as he held the burner phone between sweaty palms. He'd tried calling Cortez three times. He still wasn't answering his calls and no text back. He tried a second number, one only four people knew. Still nothing. Lex wiped his forehead with the sleeve of his shirt, heart thudding like bass. If Cortez wasn't answering, it meant something. It meant Lex was already a dead man walking.

He looked around the dingy room, suddenly aware of how cheap it all was. The stained carpet. The flickering bulb. The cinderblock walls that had felt secure now felt like a tomb. He considered running. But where? Cortez had reach. Maverick had eyes. There was nowhere in this city that wouldn't eventually swallow him. He set the burner down. Lit a cigarette with shaky fingers. Exhaled smoke like a prayer.

He decided to go outside and get some air. The alley was quiet, dumpsters reeking of rot and rat piss. Lex knew the trick was to never let your nerves show. That's why he stepped out of the back office acting as if he owned the stink in the alley and the dying night itself. The door banged shut behind him, muffling the sound of the poker game and the low, desperate voices that came with it. He took one stride onto the warped cement, sucked in air thick with dumpster rot and the sweet, metallic scent of rust, and exhaled slow. He was sweating, but not due to heat; it came from the three separate conversations he'd just had on three burner phones in the last forty minutes. He flicked his cigarette into the dark and watched its ember arc through the shadow appearing as a warning shot.

A scurrying sound in the heap of trash bags—rat, probably, or possum, but it got his hackles up anyway. He reached for the next cigarette, tapping the pack twice on his palm, but his hands wouldn't stop shaking. He told himself it was just the caffeine, or the nicotine, or the fact that he hadn't slept more than four hours in a week. He stood with his back flat against the wall, letting the bricks leech the heat from his spine, watching the alley's mouth for any sign of movement.

He didn't see the shadow by the loading dock at first. He was too busy remembering all the ways he'd fucked up. A clicking of boot heels brought him back. Slow, steady, echoing off the concrete. Lex straightened, tried to look casual, but his gut twisted, and his tongue stuck to the roof of his mouth. "You lost?" he called out, voice louder than he intended. "Ain't no back entrance for pizza delivery."

The silhouette drifted closer, picking up the glow from the overhead lamp. Broad-shouldered, moving with a kind of fluid inevitability. Black jacket, black jeans, black cap pulled low. Lex felt a bead of sweat cut down his cheek. He was ready to yell again, to bluff or threaten or maybe just run, but by then it was too late.

The man—Diego—lifted a hand, and the flash of the weapon was almost polite. A small, matte-black pistol not even aimed high. The first shot made a sound like a branch snapping under snow. Lex felt the impact in his chest, a hot, blossoming punch that made his arms go numb. The second shot, a fraction of a second after, clipped his shoulder and spun him sideways, crashing him back against the trash bags. He slid to the ground, legs folding awkwardly underneath him, his vision tunneling as blood bubbled up in his throat.

He tried to say something, maybe beg, maybe curse, but all that came out was a wet cough. He looked up and saw Diego approach, cool as a surgeon, eyes flat and reflective. He stepped over him, with one gloved hand, Diego reached into Lex's jacket and seized the burner phone from his pocket. Lex tried to grab for it—reflex, nothing more—but his hand failed him. Diego dropped the phone onto the pavement, raised his boot, and drove the heel down until it cracked and scattered.

Lex's world collapsed to a pinpoint, the alley narrowing until it was just a smear of light and shadow. He watched Diego turn and disappear around the corner, no hurry, no need to look back. Lex heard the faint rattle of a car starting up, then nothing at all. By the time the rats emerged from behind the dumpster, Lex's blood was blooming on the concrete like oil, and his body was already cooling in the night.

The Setup

Chapter Ten

The spa was a picture of peace but operated with the influence of power. Tucked behind a frosted-glass entrance in downtown Houston, the spot was one of Genevieve's off-the-books luxuries—invite-only, no walk-ins, no names on the door. Lavender steam curled through the air concealing secrets. The place smelled of eucalyptus and expensive lies. Pilar didn't think twice when she received the invite from Genevieve. She was too flattered.

An attendant handed Pilar a robe so plush

it nearly erased memory of her own skin, then led her down a corridor lined with glass tiles that rippled with shifting light. The air had a taste: orchid and ozone, violets bruised with something darker. Somewhere, a water feature played an artificial creek on loop, but even the trickling through hidden speakers felt designer. Genevieve was already waiting in the private suite, lounging in a cream wrap, her hair up, her bare face a masterwork of minimalism and effortless, like wealth just lived in her skin. She stood when Pilar entered, arms open, voice warm.

"Pilar, love. You made it."

"Of course! Thank you for having me," Pilar said, trying to keep her tone casual but grateful. This wasn't just a spa invite—this was a summon.

Genevieve handed her a flute—crystal, cucumber, the faintest wisp of juniper. "Just us today. Somewhere neutral. Where we can talk without noise and the constraints of the workplace."

She nodded toward the heated lounge chairs. They sat with their feet soaking in warm stone basins, mist dancing over the surface. The music was soft, almost forgettable, but it filled every corner like a bodyguard. Genevieve made small talk at first. Work. The city. Pilar answered politely, but her nerves were on full alert. She watched Genevieve more than she listened—clocked every glance toward the security panel, every silent scan of the room.

"You've been glowing lately," Genevieve said. Smooth. Sharp. Measured.

Pilar smiled, trying to play it cool. "I hadn't noticed but thank you."

"I'm sure you have," Genevieve replied. "Don't downplay yourself. People are talking. Word travels fast in this city."

Pilar exhaled. "Hopefully, they're talking good things."

Genevieve didn't blink. "You're getting close to a man named Brice, right?"

The mention of his name hit the air like a slap. Pilar was completely caught off guard but tried to recover. "Yeah. We've been spending a lot of time together. He's different."

Genevieve leaned in slightly. "Different how?"

"He makes me feel special," Pilar said quietly. "Like the world could be mine."

Genevieve's expression didn't waver. But her smile tightened just enough to shift the energy. "How much do you know about him?"

Pilar hesitated. "Enough."

Genevieve nodded, turning the response

over like a gemstone in her palm. "When it comes to a man, it's never enough."

An attendant slid in, topped off the water, added herbs that turned the steam pale blue. The room stayed quiet, the pressure building.

"I look out for my people, and I consider you to be one of them," Genevieve said. "I've seen too many get swept up by something new, shiny, only to find out it's the same old trap. If Brice is what he says he is, fine. But if he's not..."

"He's not like that." Pilar said it quick, almost too quick. "I'd know."

Genevieve's hand found hers, nails painted the color of dried blood. "You're smart, but love can make us all a little stupid. Trust me, I've been there."

"I can't imagine you ever being stupid at anything."

"That's 'cause I survived it," Genevieve said. "I learned from it, so the scars have all healed."

"Your life just seems perfect. But I guess nothing is perfect," Pilar shrugged.

Silence fell. Not awkward for Genevieve. Just heavy. Then, without warning. "You ever think about disappearing?"

Pilar blinked. "What...No. Besides, I don't have any place to go."

"That's not true." Genevieve swirled the last of her drink, then set the glass down with a soft click. "If you ever needed to vanish, really vanish, I could arrange it. No questions, no debts. I hope you know that. If you had to vanish. No goodbyes, no second chances. Could you do it?"

"Why would I want to vanish?"

Genevieve traced the rim of her glass. "'Cause this city chews people up. And it don't always spit them back out in one piece."

Pilar's phone buzzed. She reached for it, froze.

Genevieve noticed. "Is that him?"

"Yeah," Pilar admitted coyly.

"Go ahead. I'm not a warden."

Pilar glanced at the message—a meme, silly and sweet. She smiled, tried to hide it. Genevieve clocked everything.

"Keep him close," Genevieve advised. "But never forget who you are when he's not around. Don't ever let someone write your story for you."

Genevieve stood, dried off with practiced grace, then looked over her shoulder. "People think the main character can't die early. But stories change really quick."

Pilar laughed nervously. "That sounds like something from a movie."

Genevieve winked. "Or maybe I wrote it myself."

They wrapped up in silence. Pilar declined the facial, Genevieve didn't. A tray of fruit came and went. They chatted, but every word had substance. This wasn't bonding. This was probing. When Genevieve finally stood to leave, she looked Pilar dead in the eye.

"I want to do this again," she said. "I see parts of me in you. I just want to make sure nobody takes that from you."

Pilar nodded, unsure what she felt. "I'd like that."

Genevieve leaned in, kissed both cheeks, and swept out like a storm with no rain, leaving behind a signature of perfume and purpose. Pilar stayed behind, unsure of what just happened. But the weight of it hung in the air long after Genevieve was gone.

The carwash off the highway looked dead—no lights, no hum, no indication it ever did real business. Just a half-lit "CLOSED" sign crooked in the window, and a busted SUV idling in the shadows.

Out here, darkness stuck like sweat, the kind that only shows up where no one dares to look twice.

If you knew what button to press under the busted neon, a low click echoed somewhere behind the steel walls. A door slid open to a hallway lined with dingy tile and the thick stink of soap, rubber, and whatever they sprayed to hide blood and bad choices.

At the back, past racks of fake cleaner and broken vacuums, a fake wall snapped open to reveal the real operation.

Dim bulb swinging. Cheap whiskey lined up like soldiers on a war-ready shelf. A beat-up pool table sat center stage; it felt so scarred it looked like it survived a shootout. Folding chairs, ashtrays loaded with half-smoked blunts, Newport cigarettes and a dusty monitor playing perimeter footage on loop made the room feel lived-in and ready for trouble.

Dre was already in the mix, feet kicked up, scrolling through a USB plugged into the security setup. Midas stood posted up in the corner, arms folded, the sleeve on his hoodie rolled to show off a gold watch and a phoenix tatted up his forearm like it was ready to fly out his skin. Renny walked in last. Cold in his eyes, colder in his breath. He didn't say a word. Just nodded. Dre didn't look up, he continued to click through photo after photo.

"Good thing you told us to set up surveillance over there, 'cause Lex Bo's gone," Dre said flat. "One of Cortez's hitters. In, out. Real clean."

"Took 'em long enough," Midas muttered, toothpick rocking from one side of his mouth to the other.

Renny didn't flinch. He leaned on the edge of the pool table, arms crossed like he was holding in fire. "Means they thought he talked. Got rattled. Now they on cleanup mode."

Midas pointed at the monitor. "You wanna see how real it got?"

Dre flipped the screen. Grainy footage lit up. A back alley. A car rolls up. Two shadows jump out. One hangs by the door, the other moves like he was born to end lives. Lex doesn't even see it coming—two silenced pops. Body hits the pavement. The shooter kneels, takes something from his pocket, stomps it, and vanishes.

"Burner," Dre said. "Snatched it before it could ring again. They ain't just silencing him. They covering every crack he might've let light through."

Renny reached into his jacket and pulled a folded piece of paper. Didn't open it at first. Just stared at it as if it had teeth. When he did unfold it, it showed a printout—creased, smudged, but still readable. An address and a block map of Fifth Ward.

"They been moving outta this spot," Renny said. "Old storefront near the scrap yard. Guns, phones, now cash. Fast moves. Clean drops. Every time we tail one of their people, the path leads back here."

Midas let out a low whistle. "Why they so bold? Ain't they worried about heat?"

Dre shook his head. "Cortez don't wait. If he put one in Lex, it's 'cause he got something bigger coming. He playing chess. We need to flip his board before he finishes the move. Do you think it's time for you to reach out to Genesis? Let him know that Maverick might've moved his bullshit to Houston."

Renny tapped the red square on the map. "Not yet. Let's gather more info. I want eyes on that spot 24/7. No movement without us knowing. Dre, hack into street cams, get timestamps. Midas, rotate your boys around. No contact, just shadows. If they peep us watching, we torch the setup and start from scratch. But until then? Ghost mode."

Dre smirked. "So, we waiting to hit?"

Renny looked up, eyes sharp as a boxcutter.

"Let 'em sweat. Let 'em wonder how deep we already cut. But when we move."

He slammed the pool table once, flat palm. "We blow the whole fuckin' door off."

Midas cracked his knuckles, itching to make noise. "Say less."

They stood there for a beat, that quiet moment right before a gun gets cocked or a plan gets deadly. The city outside felt like it was holding its breath. Renny folded the paper, slid it back in his jacket. His eyes lingered on the looping video of the alley, the cold way Lex hit the pavement.

"He wanna play shadow games?" he said finally, voice low and lethal.

"Then let's show him who runs the dark."

Diego moved as silently and quickly as a ghost, blood on his boots. The service station bathroom was dead silent except for the low hum of flickering lights and the distant groan of freeway traffic. The tiles were cracked, walls stained from years of piss and neglect, but it worked—nobody checked for killers in places like this.

He peeled off the gloves slow. Left first. Then

right. Snap. Snap. Dropped 'em into a thick black contractor bag already swallowing evidence: burner phone still on airplane mode, hoodie with the tag snatched out, boots damp with alley water and regret. No hesitation, no second glance.

Three wipes came next—travel pack, surgical grade. One for the wheel. One for the shift. One for the dash. Clean. Precise. Cold. He zipped the bag, tucked a brick inside like a final blessing, and slung it over his shoulder. Then he froze, dead still inside the stall, ears peeled for footsteps. Nothing but the soft moan of Houston night pressing in from the streets.

The door creaked open with a push of his knuckle. He strolled out casual, eyes scanning for bystanders. SUV still idling by the dumpsters, windows fogged. He parked two blocks over near a construction site.

When he felt the calm settle in his chest, he moved. Inside the shell of a future luxury condo, he found a rusted barrel already tattooed with cigarette burns. He dumped the bag inside, drenched it in lighter fluid, and struck a match from a diner three states away. He watched the flame stutter, then rise. Plastic curled. Rubber popped. The burner phone cracked loud like a bone splitting. Diego watched it all turn to ash, then turned his back. Smoke clung to his clothes like a lover with no boundaries.

The streets welcomed him with that same old grime. Sky overhead was bruised and glowing, half violence, half luminous. He passed a laundromat full of stacked chairs and lost clothes, a pawn shop sign flickering like it owed rent, and a busted payphone that hadn't rung in years. Kept his head low. Feet steady. Vibe unreadable. Turned down a side street where a stray pit-bull growled at shadows and a couple cussed each other out in broken Spanish. A left onto another block took him to the bar—no name, just a faded-ass rooster sprayed on cinderblock.

Inside was all nicotine breath and sticky floors. The light was jaundiced. The vibe was *stay quiet or get checked.* He sat far end of the bar, no TV, no small talk. The bartender slid him a mezcal before he even opened his mouth. White hair. Steel in her spine. She'd seen his kind before and didn't flinch. That's why he came here. First sip hit like a silent gunshot. Smoky. Sharp. Burned clean. Two stools down, a dude in a windbreaker tried to lock eyes. Diego didn't bite. Names made you known. Known got you dead. His fresh burner vibrated. New phone bought cash an hour ago. He didn't flip it over. Just glanced at the preview.

Cortez: *Next assignment coming. Stay low.*

He downed the last of his drink. Tapped the bar once. The bartender refilled without a word. Loyalty built in silence. He drained the second glass. Wiped his mouth. Dropped cash for three. Then he stepped back out into the dark, mezcal blooming through his chest like ignition. Three blocks east. North at the busted stoplight. Down an alley with no witnesses but rats. He was already erasing the footprints behind him. He was smoke. Just silence. And Diego was just getting warmed up.

Laying The Trap

Chapter Eleven

Bass thumped low through the velvet walls, lights melted over glass like honey, and stacks of cash passed hands with the rhythm of whispered confessions in The Garden Room. But Genevieve wasn't here for the show tonight. She was hunting. From the upstairs booth, she watched it all. Her heels clicked quiet against the marble; her gaze ice-cold behind custom strip lashes. She wasn't studying the dancers or the men showcasing their $5000 bottles. Her eyes were locked on two women: Pilar and Shay.

Genevieve leaned against the one-way glass of the mezzanine suite, arms folded, watching her two best assets circle each other below. One was a chess prodigy in sequins, the other a wolf in borrowed sheep's clothing. She was not afraid to lose either, but she would not lose both. One might be loyal. The other? A problem waiting to happen.

There'd been no fanfare to this test—no labels, memos or instructions. Just a last-minute shift in schedule and a notorious out-of-town client with cartel whispers on his name rumored to be involved with arms trafficking. Genevieve sent Pilar in solo. Told Shay to observe and take notes. That was it. The rest? The trap.

Pilar entered the VIP suite with an air of authority that commanded attention. Her black silk dress complimented her figure with a precision that was both professional yet effortlessly sexy. Her hair, meticulously pinned up like art, jewelry quiet but intentional. Words were unnecessary as her presence was a force, a silent storm that swept through the room with undeniable impact. She handed off her phone at the door, scanned the room, and took mental notes as if she was trained by the feds. No last names. No over-talking. No slipping. You could drop this woman in any diplomatic reception from Caracas to Berlin and she'd fit in seamlessly. Pilar poured drinks with distance. Gave the client respect but kept her walls high. Every move was clean. No flinch. No fear.

Shay? Sloppy. Showed up late wearing a loud *look at me* red pantsuit. Hung in the hallway too long, leaning in like a nosy cousin. Eyes darting. Obviously eavesdropping. Phone out scrolling, texting, which was a blatant breach of protocol. Genevieve clocked it all. Shay was clueless and didn't see the wireless camera embedded in the thermostat or the silent observer perched in the mezzanine. She didn't know that every move-ment was being logged and time-stamped, not just by management, but by the client's own se-curity detail. Especially the one built like a re-tired MMA champ who studied her every twitch, ready and waiting to pounce.

When Pilar noticed Shay peering in, instead of reacting, she subtly shifted her body, block-ing Shay's line of sight, and kept it fluid. By the end of the evening, the client left satisfied. Pilar thanked him, maintaining her professionalism. Shay stood on the edge of the action, looking like she expected a trophy. Genevieve didn't give her one.

Later, behind the back bar, Pilar was restocking glasses when Shay rolled up.

"So... how do you think it went?" Shay asked, trying to sound easy breezy.

"Smooth," Pilar said without turning. "Client left happy. Which means I did my job."

Shay leaned in. "You don't think it was weird Genevieve sent you in solo with him? Word is he moves heavy. I'm talking cartel connections. Guns."

Pilar shrugged. "And, what does that have to do with me?"

"I'm just saying—not everybody comfortable around those type of dudes, especially being alone with them. Maybe she was testing you to see if you could swim with sharks."

Pilar sighed. "I wasn't alone, now, was I? You were there as my shadow. So, maybe she was testing you."

Shay became defensive. "Me? What for? I ain't done nothin' that would make her test me."

"Then you good." Pilar gave a slow smile. "But you know Genevieve sees everything. Even the shit you think you hiding."

Later that night, Genevieve stepped past the valets out front. Shay was by the curb, bent over her phone, thumbs flying. Her expression screamed nervous. Her body said guilty. Genevieve didn't say a word at first. Just watched. Then Shay noticed her and flinched. Tried to smile. Failed.

"Everything cool?" Genevieve asked, voice syrup slow.

Shay forced it out. "Yeah... just tired. Long night."

"Mmhmm." Genevieve nodded. "Longest nights usually got the loudest consequences. Get home safe."

She didn't move until Shay disappeared down the block, phone still glued to her hand. Then she made the call.

"Keep eyes on Shay," she said, voice low but final. "I'm getting snake tendencies. Don't touch her yet. I want to see who she reports to."

Renny's feet hit the tarmac with the softest of thuds, the hush of the private airstrip in Westchester absorbing his arrival like a secret. The sky was gunmetal gray. The Hudson looked ready to swallow a man whole. There were no handlers, no badge-flashing TSA, just a curt nod from the charter pilot and a black SUV parked down by the gate idling at the far end of the runway.

He popped his collar against the wind, caught sight of the SUV. Tinted windows. Engine running, the passenger-side window slid down just enough for Renny to catch a stone face—mid-40s, piercing eyes, silence on standby. Renny gave a half-nod and slid into the backseat without a word. No questions asked. Just the city pulling him back in. The ride was quiet. Thirty miles of blurred exits. Renny didn't sleep. He didn't need to. Not sleeping just sharpened the edge.

By the time they pulled up to Genesis's building, it was pushing midnight. A mid-rise tucked off the avenue, the kind of place where the doorman had orders to forget faces. Renny stepped out, scanned the block—nothing but damp pavement and tension in the air. Thumbprint entry. Elevator that moved smooth but gave the vibe of a trap door. Mirrors everywhere, reflecting a man who knew too much to flinch.

The penthouse doors slid open with a hush. Genesis was posted at the far end like a king with war on his mind expecting the storm. He stood with his hands in the pockets of a flawless black cashmere sweatsuit, the kind of leisurewear that cost more than most people's mortgages. The cut of his jawline remained strikingly defined, rugged as ever, yet chiseled with intent, as if crafted to make a statement, rather than being a mere product of nature.

"Didn't think you'd show without a heads up," Genesis said, tone direct and built for control.

"If I called, you'd tell me stay my ass in Houston. I needed your eyes, not your advice," Renny said, ducking under the arm Genesis extended like a gate. No hugs. No dap. Just stillness and a climb up the spiral staircase lined with money and memories— walls with original Basquiat's and an entire hall of family portraits that looked like a study in deliberate vulnerability.

Renny let his eyes linger on the pictures of Genesis's wife, Talisa—still beautiful, even after what Arnez put her through. Amir, full of promise. Little Desi, Little Genie. And Genevieve, back before the rebrand, when Nichelle still showed in her smile.

Upstairs, the office was all power and precision. Obsidian desk. Shelves stacked with first editions and trophies that could kill a man. Genesis nodded at a chair. Renny ignored it, drifted to the window. City lights smudged by fog. Everything looked soft from up high, but they both knew better.

"So, talk," Genesis said. "You didn't come all this way because you missed me."

Renny waited until the whiskey was poured—decanted from a bottle shaped like a grenade. He took a sip. Let it burn.

"Maverick got new hands moving in Houston," he said. "One of 'em's named Cortez Mercer. Might be ex-military. Might just be a street general with a passport and a code. I can't confirm, but my gut tells me, he's pushing from your side. Quiet. Strategic. We wait, he cuts deep."

Genesis didn't blink. "Maverick don't play chess. He flips the whole board."

"Exactly." Renny nodded. "That's why I think he might got eyes on Genevieve. Watching her. Maybe trying to use her to get to you."

Genesis's grip tightened just enough for the veins in his hand to show. "He believes she's my weak spot."

Renny nodded. "Maverick ain't dumb. He's looking for bloodlines to exploit."

Genesis stared out the window, city haze painting his face in war light. "How sure are you about this Cortez and his connection to Maverick?"

"I only recently got confirmation of their direct association, which is why I'm here. I got eyes on his orbit. 24-hour surveillance. Cortez is a slippery nigga, but no one's perfect. He gon' fuck up."

"Who else knows?"

"Just me. Dre. Midas. And now you." Renny paused. "I ain't told Genevieve. Don't want her stressed or distracted."

Genesis smirked. "My little sister always sees more than she let on."

"Yeah. That's what scares me."

They drank. The silence between them wasn't peace—just two wolves breathing in sync.

"Send me everything you got on Cortez," Genesis said. "I'll dig from this side. We coordinate. If he moves on either of ours, we bury him. Together."

Renny set his glass down. "While you're at it, look into a chick named Shay. She works at The Garden Room. Genevieve getting a weird vibe about her."

Genesis raised an eyebrow. "Your wife is usually right about people. I remember when she warned me about Coco."

Renny nodded. "I know."

Genesis leaned forward. "Send me her file. I'll find out if she needs to be handled. Maverick is even more resourceful and brazen than I thought if he's trying to make a move through Genevieve?"

Renny's eyes narrowed. "I think he looking for the one move that'll break you."

Genesis finished the whiskey in one swallow. Set the glass down slow. "If he touches my sister, I'll put him in the dirt with my own hands."

"If he come near my wife, I'll get to him first," Renny promised.

Years of tension, bloodlines, and backroom deals consumed the room. Genesis stood, walked to the bar. "Pour another?" he asked. "I mean if we about to go to war, might as well toast to family."

Renny agreed. They raised glasses. No words, just eye contact that said everything. To family.

When Renny left, hours later, the elevator swallowed him up the same way it had delivered him—soundlessly, without a trace. The only evidence of the meeting was the empty bottle on the windowsill, the faintest scent of smoke in the air, and two men who'd just signed a silent contract. War was coming. And this time, nobody was walking away clean.

Doomsday

Chapter Twelve

The sound of her assistant's shoes on the marble shattered the silence. It was a warning shot, resonating through the glass and tinted stainless steel gallery of Genevieve's office. Sam hovered in the entrance of the double doors, clutching a tablet to his chest, his mouth taut.

"Genevieve," he said, voice tight as a wire. "Cortez Mercer is here to see you."

She didn't look up right away; she finished the line she was reading, let the words settle. "What the hell does he want?" not really a question, more of a reflex. Genevieve's spine stiffened—but only for a second, like a snake coiling under silk.

"He only said it was related to business," Sam informed her.

Genevieve set her tablet down with a deliberate click, her wrist moving elegantly yet dismissive, before uncrossing her legs. "Fine. Send him up," she said.

Sam nodded and slid out, retreating with urgency. Genevieve leaned back, exhaling with annoyance. She adjusted the cuff of her blouse and reached for her gloss like she was loading a round into the chamber. As she smoothed it on, she mentally prepared herself to be face-to-face with a man rumored to make witnesses vanish without a trace.

The elevator opened with a muted chime. Cortez stepped in like he'd just bought the building. Tailored black suit. Fresh cut. The scar on his face didn't make him less handsome—it made him dangerous in a way most men pretended to be. His smile didn't touch his eyes. Those were hunter's eyes.

"Genevieve O'Neal," he said, voice smooth as aged rum. "Had to come meet the woman bold enough to run this city and whisper my name in the process."

Genevieve rested in her chair, fingers steepled. "I don't whisper, Mr. Mercer. If I'm asking about you, it's because I intend to find out what you won't volunteer." She let her gaze rest on his face, daring him to break eye contact first. He didn't.

"Respect," Cortez said, and it wasn't sarcastic. He took her in, not in the leering way most men did, but the way a chess player evaluates the opening of a game. He strolled the length of her office, not quite circling her but close enough, pausing at the photos on the built-in bookcase. He reached out, touched the edge of a frame—a picture of Genevieve, Renny, and Elijah on a beach somewhere humid, all three in sunglasses and grinning like they'd just pulled off a billion dollar heist.

"I figured I'd save you the trouble and allow you to speak directly to the source. Always preferred honesty over speculation."

Genevieve stood, walked toward him. Close. Controlled. "Then let's not dance around it. I'm very protective of my people. Especially one named Pilar. She's been seen getting close to a man named Brice. You wouldn't know anything about that, would you?"

A brief moment slipped by. His eyes darted quickly before he flashed a broader grin, showcasing his white teeth and a troublesome past. "Brice," he mused, "sounds familiar."

"Don't play with me." Her voice cut razor straight. "If he works for you—if you're using him to get close to my business—we'll have a problem."

Cortez's expression flickered just a shade, the way a boxer's stance shifts when he realizes the other guys left-handed. He tilted his head, the gleam in his eyes shifting from amused to intrigued. "Let's just say... if I had someone on the inside, I'd make sure they didn't even know who they were working for."

Genevieve double downed. "Then let me be clear. Pilar is under my protection. Whatever game you're playing, leave her out of it. Or you'll find out why people in this city know better than to cross me."

For a moment, nothing moved. The air between them felt ionized, a pre-storm charge. Then—Cortez's mask slipped. The smile vanished. "You want me to stay away from Pilar. Say it."

"I want you to stay away from every single person who works for me," Genevieve said. "And if you don't, you'll wish you had."

Cortez straightened, nodded once, as if he'd just been given a riddle with two possible answers and found both correct. Then, almost as an afterthought, he said, "That's why you married a man like Renny? To keep your enemies guessing?"

Genevieve laughed, the sound low and unhurried. She stepped closer, her perfume hitting him like a stray bullet. "I married Renny because sometimes a queen needs a knight who isn't afraid of blood. But don't fool yourself. I don't need anyone to do my fighting for me. Oh, and thank you for confirming that you're my enemy."

Cortez put both hands on the back of the guest chair, eyes narrowing. "That a threat?"

"A guarantee, that's all I make," she answered, level and cold.

He let go of the chair and drifted closer, into her personal space, once again taking in her scent, it was almost hypnotic—something sharp, citrus. "You don't seem to be the kind of woman who likes to get her hands dirty," he said softly.

She grinned, teeth showing now. "I run a club, not a monastery. My hands have been dirty since I was old enough to know what dirt was for."

The silence between them pulsed like a live wire. Then Cortez produced a card, matte black, no logo, just a phone number embossed in silver. He set it on the corner of her desk, then stepped back.

"In case you ever want a real conversation," he said. This time, the smile almost reached his eyes. He turned, walked out, not even bothering to glance at Sam, who'd been standing rigid by the door the whole time.

The elevator doors shut behind him with a soft hydraulic sigh, and then the office was quiet again. Genevieve picked up the card, studied it. She knew better than to call, but she also knew better than to throw it away. She slid it into her top drawer, next to the small, gleaming handgun that Genesis had gifted her before moving to Houston. She let out a breath she hadn't realized she'd been holding, then sat back down, already thinking ten moves ahead.

Following the meeting with Genesis in New York, they concurred that he should accelerate the dismantling of Cortez's organization to prevent any future retaliation. This was precisely what Renny and his team were executing.

Renny whispered, crouched low behind a rusted dumpster as the wind kicked dust through the chain-link fence. Dre and Midas flanked him, gloved up, masked down. The warehouse loomed like a forgotten fortress—two guards at the door, a third pacing the far side, armed. They scanned the perimeter of the warehouse one more time. It was a slab of industrial rot, abandoned but not empty, its windows patched with cardboard and plastic, the roof sagging with decades of wet. And yet, despite the camouflage of decay, the place bristled with intent: motion sensor lights, the whine of a backup generator, the slow orbit of an unblinking red security camera high above the loading bay.

They'd mapped every entrance and every camera angle. They knew the routines—how the guards rotated, how often the third man on the far side stepped out to piss in the alley, how each shift overlapped by seven minutes exactly, a margin that spoke of management-level para-noia. Every detail accounted for, save the margin for error that made a job like this less of a science and more of a story told in blood and dollar signs.

The wind keened through the chain link as Renny raised two fingers—a silent signal—and Dre nodded back, already rolling his shoulders, already visualizing the silent sprint to cover. Midas was a statue, all stillness but for the flicker of his eyes, which never left the warehouse's battered door. "You know the drill. Quiet," Renny murmured, not so much a command as a benediction. He started the countdown. "Three... two... one."

Dre moved first, fast and silent, crossing the open ground in a blink, his boots muffled by the dead leaves and dust. He was on the first guard before the man even registered a threat, his arm coiling around the neck, the other hand clamping hard over the mouth. The guard's knees buckled, but Dre bore him down slow, a dancer lowering a partner in the world's least romantic dip. A muffled gasp, the slackening of limbs, then Dre dragged the body behind a stack of warped pallets, face pale above the black of his mask. Renny waited just long enough to verify the fall before he and Midas broke cover, splitting left and right.

Renny vaulted the low concrete barrier, boots hitting the asphalt with a dull report. The second guard turned at the sound, eyes wide, mouth forming an Oh that was stillborn—Renny closed the gap and brought his elbow up, finding the soft hinge of the man's jaw. The blow carried all the weight of every bad night Renny had ever lived, and the guard hit the ground hard, out cold or close enough. On the far side, Midas went wide, circling left with a Glock in hand. He stalked the perimeter, using shadow like a cloak.

The third guard was still fumbling with his zipper, back to the alley, when Midas put the muzzle of his pistol to the base of the man's skull. The guard stiffened, but Midas leaned in, voice level, "Don't yell." The guard nodded, then promptly pissed himself, standing rigid while Midas zip-tied his wrists and shoved him into the garbage pile with a "Stay." Three guards, three non-lethal takedowns; finesse, not carnage, at least for now.

They regrouped at the side door, Dre already fitting the wedge into the frame, Midas fishing for the flashbang in his jacket. Renny flattened himself against the cinderblock and whispered, "On my mark." He counted down with his hand, then nodded: Midas pulled the pin, cracked the door open a sliver, and rolled the grenade over the threshold. A half-second of silence. Then the flashbang ignited, the world inside the warehouse going white-hot and deaf for a full two seconds. An explosion of shouts, curses, and the metallic clang of bodies stumbling into steel shelves and each other.

They poured in, Dre low and fast, Midas

right behind with gun ready, Renny dropping to one knee and squeezing off two quick shots: both landed, both men folding over, hands clutching at their thighs, not fatal but more than enough to end resistance. Inside the warehouse was a geometry of chaos—rows of stacked crates, card tables littered with cash, burner phones, and pill bottles, the air now thick with gunpowder and the faint, sweet tang of opiates. A handful of men, all dressed in the off-brand athletic wear of low-level muscle, scrambled for cover, one diving behind a crate and another making for the spiral stair leading to the mezzanine.

Renny tracked them, methodical, not wasting bullets: pop, pop, another man dropped, his hand spasming and sending a spray of cash fluttering through the air. Midas covered the back, eyes always on the exits. When a man dove for a duffel at his feet, Midas put a round through the bag, the bullet traversing flesh and nylon equally. The man howled, crumpled, and Midas advanced, stepping over the fresh blood with professional detachment. Dre was already at the main office, using the butt of his pistol to shatter the glass. He reached through, unlatched the door, and held it open for Renny, who entered with a slow, deliberate step, as if daring anyone inside to try him.

The office was less a command center than a disaster zone—a battered computer tower on the floor, a folding table doubling as a desk, paperwork scattered everywhere. A single man sat behind the table, hands up, eyes wild. "You don't want this," the man stammered, eyes darting between Renny and the pistol. Renny didn't answer. He went straight for the laptop, saw it was still logged in, the screen alive with a spreadsheet of names and numbers. He yanked the power cord, tucked the machine under his arm, and scanned the desk for anything else of value. A ledger, the entries in code but the amounts unmistakable: tens of thousands, hundreds, all flowing from the same three initials—CMG. Cortez Mercer Group.

He was about to leave when he noticed the phone—burner, pocketed it and headed back out, signaling Dre to sweep the storage office for anything they missed. "Grab everything. Burn the rest," Renny ordered, voice flat but cold. Dre and Midas worked quickly: laptops, ledgers, stacks of cash, all dumped into the duffels they brought. The rest—pills, guns, unsold product—they doused with acetone and lit, a controlled burn that would erase everything but the concrete slab. Outside, the sound of sirens began to build, distant but closing.

They exited the warehouse through the loading bay, Midas already on the phone to the fire dispatcher, reporting a "possible meth lab fire" at the address. By the time anyone official arrived, the place would be a shell, the evidence a smear of ash and acrid smoke.

Dre parked the van in the alley, Renny and Midas in the back. The adrenaline bled off in stages, leaving behind the metallic taste of triumph and near-miss. Renny unlocked the phone, scanned the messages, reading between the lines: the real target wasn't the cash, wasn't the product. It was Maverick, and the pipeline of information he represented. They'd just severed that artery. But Renny knew well enough cut off one head, the body grows another. Always does.

He opened the laptop, started scrolling. Dre watched him in the rearview, waiting for the verdict. "Well?" Dre asked.

"We get what we came for?" Renny thumbed through the spreadsheets, his mind already assembling the next move. "We got more than we came for," he said. And for the first time all night, he let himself believe it.

Smoke & Mirrors

Chapter Thirteen

Pilar's Friday began like any other: a double at The Garden Room, a parade of tech execs, drunken ballplayers, and women in thousand-dollar heels trying to get chosen. She was adjusting her hoop earring in the brass mirror near the exit when the Bentley coupe pulled up—black-on-black, engine humming like sin. The kind of car that made the whole block stop breathing.

Brice stepped out, duffel in one hand, single red rose in the other. "No club tonight," he said with that crooked grin. "Pack your shit. You're mine for the weekend."

Pilar started to protest—she had plans, she had work—but he stepped in close, brushed his thumb across her bottom lip, and said. "Just trust me."

He pressed the rose into her hand. The thorns on the rose? Already trimmed.

Ninety minutes later, she found herself, barefoot, glowing and giddy on the tarmac at the airport, climbing the steps to a private jet, champagne flute in hand, wind playing with the loose tendrils of her hair. No TSA. No delays. Just Brice's hand on the small of her back and the hush of real power.

"You can sleep if you want," he offered. She didn't want to. Not even close. He let her cue up whatever playlist she liked, so she put on some Summer Walker. Then he curled up beside her on the leather sofa, eyes tracing her silhouette. Every glance said *she's mine*.

They landed in Jacksonville as the sky bled orange. A black Escalade stood waiting, the driver holding a sign that read **"B + P"**. You would've thought they were royalty. They didn't talk on the drive, didn't need to—Brice's hand on her thigh said everything.

They arrived at the Ritz-Carlton, Amelia Island and it was opulence wrapped in whispers: marble floors, gold keys, bellmen that didn't blink when Pilar stumbled into the lobby, tipsy giggling in Brice's arms.

Their suite on the eleventh floor was a study in excess—Oceanfront. three rooms, two balconies, floor-to-ceiling glass walls that made the Atlantic look close enough to taste, and that it belonged to them. A soaking tub the size of her last bedroom. Pilar stepped onto the terrace and just stared. Long lines of moonlight knifed through the waves, the horizon a bruised line of purple and flame. Champagne already chilled, strawberries in a crystal bowl, a gift bag on the bed with tissue paper spilling

She opened it and inside she found a silk slip dress in her size, pale blue, barely-there. The kind of dress you only wear when you've stopped asking for permission. There was a note:

Wear it for me tonight. — B.

She laughed, then cried a little, not sure if it was joy or fear. She'd never belonged to anyone's future before. She'd never been wanted so perfectly.

Brice was on the balcony when she came out, hair loose and wild, dress clinging to her like water, he turned to stone. He just watched her, eyes heavy.

"You serious?" she asked, voice low, as Brice had her feeling like she was on some Pretty Woman type shit, without even being a pro.

He closed the distance with three steps, pulled her in his arms, sprinkling kisses on the side of her neck. "Deadass."

Dinner was beachside, under a private white canopy. Lanterns swayed in the ocean breeze. Firepits crackled at each corner. No menu—just courses Brice picked without hesitation. Oysters. Lobster tail. Steak laced with chimichurri that cut sharp and clean. He fed her, watched her, wiped butter from her lip. The staff disappeared after the second course.

He asked about her dreams—not the easy kind, the real ones.

"What would you do if you could walk away from all this? No limits."

She told him about the bakery in Savannah. The house with the peach trees. Kids. A dog. Quiet Sundays reading the paper.

He didn't laugh. He listened.

He told her about growing up on the edge, about how he'd hustled for every dollar, how trust was a currency rarer than gold. Then Brice gazed deep in her yes, going all the way in to guarantee Pilar would be completely under his spell. "I always knew I was meant for more," he said. "But I didn't know what that meant until now, being here with you."

She wanted to believe him. Maybe she already did.

After dinner, Brice lifted her off the sand, carrying her back to the suite—like even her footsteps deserved protecting. Undressed her slow, as if she was a gift he hadn't earned yet. They made love with the balcony doors cracked open, the ocean crashing applause beneath them. He was gentle, almost reverent. Every kiss said you're safe, every touch said I want you, and Pilar let herself believe those feelings were real because her heart yearned for it.

She woke past midnight to the sound of the ocean and the space beside her empty. The sheets were cool, and she rolled into them, reaching, unsettled and already missing the weight of him. She sat up, pulled his T-shirt over her head, and padded barefoot toward the soft light bleeding through the balcony glass.

She heard his voice first—low, urgent. Then her name.

"Yeah. She's with me now. Nah, she don't

know. That's why I'm playing it soft. I told Cortez I'd handle it."

That name. Cortez.

The air changed. The spell broke. Pilar froze, the bottom dropped out of her stomach. Cortez. The name hit like a slap, a warning shot.

"She's all the way in." Brice kept talking, lower now, words slick with confidence. "Tell Mav the job's getting done. If she asks questions, I'll pivot. She don't suspect a thing."

The room tilted. Her chest tightened.

Every laugh. Every kiss. Every "trust me"—a setup.

Everything after that was white noise. Pilar stood rooted to the floor. She wanted to scream, to storm out onto the balcony and demand answers, but she didn't. She shut her eyes, steadied her breath, and let the anger crystallize into something sharper, cleaner. The man she'd just decided to trust—maybe even love—was a lie. Or part of one.

She backed away from the balcony, teeth clenched to stop the shaking. Her feet moved on their own, carrying her back to bed. She curled into herself beneath the sheets, heart hammering loud enough to drown out the waves, and waited for Brice to return.

Pilar heard the metallic click of the balcony door, footsteps followed as he came back inside. He slid into bed, his hand gentle on her hip, thumb tracing lazy circles on her skin, kissing her shoulder.

"Sorry, I had to take that," he whispered.

She kept her eyes closed. Played asleep. He brushed her hair off her cheek, kissed her temple, and even then, knowing what she knew, Pilar still felt the old ache, the impossible hope that maybe he was different.

Pilar continued to lay there for hours, awake and wired. One moment, her insides felt like steel, but the very next, she wanted to cry herself to sleep from a broken heart. She'd been fooled before—but never like this. Pilar began rehearsing how she should confront him, demanding the truth, prepared to risk it all. Or would it serve her better to say nothing, pretend, and use whatever time she had to figure out what Cortez wanted—and why Brice had picked her. Either way, the next move was hers. Now that she knew what Brice was, the question was, what was she going to do about it.

The master suite was dim, lit by a single candle throwing shadows across high-thread-count sheets and bare skin. The soft scent of vanilla lingered, cut with the faintest breeze drifting in from the wraparound terrace—warm night air wrapped in jasmine and danger. The danger lingering in Houston was left outside, if only for the night because in here, it was all slowed breath and body heat.

Genevieve was beneath Renny, her legs wrapped around his waist like she belonged there. Like she'd always belonged there. Her nails scraped gently down his back, leaving faint trails that burned and begged for more. Renny groaned low in his throat, biting back the sound as he pressed deeper into her, one hand gripping the back of her thigh, the other stroking slow down the side of her waist.

"Damn," he whispered against her neck, voice husky. "You tryna take all of me tonight?"

Genevieve smiled through a breathless moan, hips rolling up to meet his. "Nah, baby... I already did."

The rhythm between them was slow, deliberate—no rush, just a quiet storm building with every grind of hips and stolen breath. Her body arched against his like a wave, soft and wild, matching his energy without breaking stride. Candlelight danced over her skin, highlighting the sheen of sweat on her collarbone, the curve of her breast, the hunger in her eyes that said *don't stop.*

Renny kissed her like he was claiming her soul—deep, wet, messy. She kissed him back with all the fire he fell in love with and all the softness he never saw coming. He loved how she tasted. Loved how she moved. Loved the way she whispered his name when it cracked off her lips like a prayer and a curse all at once.

He flipped her onto her stomach, dragging her hips back into him, slow and steady. Her breath caught in her throat as she looked over her shoulder, eyes heavy with heat.

"You sure you can handle me like this?" she teased.

Renny leaned in, his voice brushing her ear. "You *mine*. I was made for this." Making love to his wife still gave him a rush, and even after all these years, it always felt like their first time.

Their bodies moved like a hidden ritual—

something sacred and untamed, meant to be sensed rather than observed. The headboard tapped the wall in time with the quiet moans and muffled gasps that filled the space between them. It wasn't about dominance. It wasn't about submission. It was about trust. It was about two people who'd fought battles side by side now finding peace in the warzone of each other.

When they finally collapsed, tangled in sweat-slick sheets and scattered kisses, Genevieve curled into his chest, one leg thrown across his hip, fingers drawing slow circles on his chest.

"You really tryna kill me tonight?" he murmured, eyes closed.

She laughed softly. "I've missed you. Missed this. We've had so much going on, that we haven't had any moments for intimacy. I needed this," she said brushing her lips on his chin.

"You're right and I apologize. We vowed to always set aside time like this for one another."

The room remained motionless for a few calm minutes. The only sounds were the faint whisper of the stars in the night sky and the sound of their breathing. Then Genevieve broke the silence.

"Cortez Mercer came to see me the other day."

Renny's eyes snapped open.

"What did you say?" the name landed like a knife. Renny stiffened, the warmth draining from his limbs, replaced with a callous, electrical vigilance.

She stayed calm. "He showed up at my office unannounced. Said he heard I was digging, trying to uncover information about him. Wanted to 'formally introduce himself.'"

"And you just now telling me?" Renny sat up slightly, looking down at her.

"Baby, we've both had so much going on. I wasn't gonna light another fuse if I didn't have to."

Renny shook his head, jaw flexing. "Genevieve, this ain't some minor player. Cortez ain't the type to just pop in for small talk. You shoulda told me."

"I handled it," she said, her tone cutting through his frustration. "He tried to finesse me, but I saw through it. I asked him flat out if Brice worked for him."

That name again. Renny's chest tightened. The crease between his eyebrows deepened. He didn't respond right away. Brice was a name with gravity, one that had started popping up in conversations that ended in either money or blood. Renny remembered the one time he'd seen him—expensive suit, hands too soft for the violence they commanded, eyes always scanning. He didn't trust men who smiled too easily.

Genevieve picked up on his mood shift immediately—she was a surgeon when it came to reading men. She continued but her voice dropping to a softer register, "Cortez deflected, but I saw the twitch in his eye. He knows who Brice is. I'm telling you... something ain't right." She paused. "I'm worried about Pilar. She left with Brice for the weekend. Took time off work. Said it was just a weekend getaway, but I think Brice is trying to pull her deeper into a trap."

"Pilar came up in the streets. She know the game," he finally said, the words brittle with forced nonchalance. "If she made a bad call, we'll catch it." He tried to sound reassuring, but Genevieve heard the hollowness beneath.

Genevieve gave a small nod and collapsed back into the pillows. "Baby, please keep an eye on Brice. Pilar might've come up in the streets, but love can have even the shrewdest woman make the wrong decision." She turned to face Renny, searching his features for the thing he wouldn't say out loud. "You sure you don't know something I don't?" her eyes were daggers: sharp, searching, unwilling to accept a lie.

Renny forced a smile. "Would I lie to you?"

Then his mind flashed back to the warehouse, to Genesis, to the name *Maverick* hanging over everything like a dark cloud. He wanted to tell her. Wanted to bring her in on what he and Genesis had mapped out, the chessboard that was already littered with fallen pieces. But not tonight. Instead, he kissed the top of her head, pulled her back into his chest.

"Don't worry, Pilar will be fine. I'll keep my eyes on Brice," he murmured.

"Thank you," Genevieve whispered, pressing a soft kiss to Renny's lips before settling into his arms. Despite the chaos, the danger that always loomed, there was still this—an escape carved out in the turmoil of the city's restless night. They stayed like that a while, the weight of the world outside forgotten, but Renny knew it wouldn't last. A tsunami was coming, and it was only a matter of time before everything tipped over the edge, as the war was near.

Shay stormed towards Cortez, looking hot and bothered. Her typical polished exterior was slipping, cracks showing in the facade. The flawless look she usually nailed felt rushed—her perfectly styled hair, thrown back in a messy bun. Her standard designer attire, only a step up from "just rolled out of bed" and screamed stress. It was obvious the pressure was starting to weigh on her, and Cortez noticed it, every little detail.

He was lounging in the back booth of an after-hours spot posing as a juice bar, his Kiton cashmere silk blazer draped over the back of his chair, a glass of bourbon sweating in front of him. Shay slid in across from him, eyes darting like she was being followed.

"You late," Cortez said.

"You always early," she shot back.

He raised an eyebrow. "What's up with the disheveled appearance, something has you nervous?"

Shay leaned in, keeping her voice low. "I think Genevieve's on to me."

Cortez took a sip, unmoved as he chewed on her words. "Did she say something?"

"Not directly. But I think a couple weeks ago she set me and Pilar up for a test?"

"What sort of test?"

"Our interactions with a client at the Garden room. Pilar seemed to pass, and I think I might've flunked miserably," Shay huffed.

"Interesting. She's smart," he said. "Too smart to come at you loud. That's why she's dangerous. Genevieve is even more intriguing than I initially thought when we met at her office," Cortez smiled.

"Wait, you went to Genevieve's office and met with her...when and why didn't you tell me?" Shay demanded to know.

"I don't recall answering to you. You work for me, not the other way around."

She paused, swallowing the lump in her throat, anxiety pressing on her chest. "Whatever, I just need to gain her trust back. You got any ideas?"

Cortez studied her. Shay was a mess of ambition and desperation—useful, but volatile.

"Don't force it," he said. "Fall back. Play the position as a loyal employee. Stay in your lane. No slick shit. No late-night calls. You play quiet, she'll think she overreacted. Pretend you're ready to follow the rules, instead of making up your own. Let her believe you scared she might let you go."

"You think that'll work?"

"Women like Genevieve need to control the room. Give her that."

Shay nodded slowly. "And Pilar?"

"She's still the target. Brice is applying pressure. Soon, she'll be all in. But keep her close. Maybe take her out for drinks and pick her brain. Because soon, we'll be ready to make our move."

Shay stood to leave. "You'll let me know when it gets... serious?"

Cortez smiled, his voice laced with warning and charm. "I advise you to move as if it's serious right now. Starting with your appearance," he strongly suggested. "Don't fumble the next part."

Shay turned to leave, but Cortez stopped her with a look. "One more thing." He pulled a wad of bills from his jacket and handed it to her. "For your loyalty."

Shay took it, consumed with uneasiness. Loyalty. That word was starting to taste like poison to her, but she was in too deep to turn back now.

After Cortez finished his drink, he went back out to his Range, phone to his ear. The call rang once before it connected.

Maverick's voice came through the other end with intensity. "Talk to me. What's the word?"

"Renny's getting bolder," Cortez said. "Hit one of our spots this week. Clean, fast, tactical.

They grabbed some records, burned the rest. Intel says it was Renny, Dre, and Midas."

"That nigga turning out to be a little more problematic than I expected him to be," Maverick grumbled.

"Genevieve's catching the scent too. I paid her a little visit, tried to keep it calm, but she's already on edge. She even asked me straight up if Brice works for us."

Maverick gave a low, dry laugh. "That woman don't miss a beat."

"She's gonna be a problem," Cortez stated.

Maverick went quiet again, the silence pressing. "Maybe it's time we send a message."

"What you thinking?"

There was no hesitation in Maverick's reply. "Maybe it's time we snatch Genevieve up. That's a message Renny and Genesis can't ignore."

"You sure you want to go that route?" Cortez asked.

"I'm done playing chess," Maverick growled. "They wanna keep poking the bear? Cool. Let's give 'em something to cry over. Snatch Genevieve. We hold her long enough for the message to land—and make sure it sticks."

Cortez leaned back, eyes on the dark skyline. "You want blood... or just fear?"

"Start with fear," Maverick said. "But if it gets messy... you know how we do."

Cortez sat back, the idea sinking in. "She is the glue between Renny and Genesis. You pull her out the frame...everything falls."

"Exactly. I already have my men working on getting Genesis's son Amir too. If we get either one or even better both, then Genesis is mine," Maverick boasted. "Time to play hardball."

Cortez stared into the silence for a long moment, then cracked his knuckles. "Alright," he said. "Let's start drawing up the plan," he agreed. "Let me handle Genevieve. I'll set up the play."

"Cool. What about Shay and the other girl?' Maverick asked.

"Shay's paranoid. Not sure if she has a legitimate reason or if Genevieve is simply playing head games with her. But she might've been clocked, however Pilar's still in pocket. Brice took her away for the weekend to make sure she's locked in," Cortez revealed.

"A'ight, I'll be looking out for the next update."

The call ended. And the war moved one step closer to home.

Chapter Fourteen

Genevieve was out the door by five after eight, as always. Today's armor was a doeskin color L'Agence "Clementine" blazer with a unique lace construction and contrasting satin lapels, paired with a lustrous white silk cowl neckline camisole, fitted laser stone washed denim jeans, a butter white VLogo signature leather belt and pointed tortoise printed calf leather stiletto pumps. Her hair in a high, sleek, loosely curled ponytail, with just enough makeup to have someone wonder if she naturally wakes up a ten or has a little cosmetic help.

Her heels were Louboutin, but she kept a pair of Nikes beneath the car seat. She had always believed in being prepared—not just for the boardroom, but for whatever the world might hurl at her between the garage and the office tower. The house was empty except for the two private security men engaged in a chess game in the guest room. They only glanced up when she strode past them, her perfume exuding an aura of power rather than sweetness. She nodded at them. They nodded back, impassive faces betraying nothing. The city was already alive and howling by the time she rolled out of the drive, the paper-white gates yawning open as if to spit her onto the street.

Genevieve made it three blocks before she felt it: the tingle at the base of her skull, the static that meant eyes were on her. She checked the rearview on instinct. There it was, a silver SUV, with windows tinted as dark as obsidian, following closely, just two car lengths behind. At first, she tried to dismiss it. Paranoia was a family inheritance, after all, and she'd spent a lifetime learning not to jump at every shadow. But the SUV stayed with her, patient as a shark. She slowed to forty in a fifty zone and watched the mirror. The SUV slowed, too, not so close as to spook her but never far enough to break the tension.

She changed lanes, ducked around a delivery van, then waited to see if the tail would reveal itself with an impatient swerve or a careless stoplight run. Instead, the SUV drifted smoothly, always two cars back, always in the rightmost lane, never in a hurry. Her phone buzzed—calendar alert. She ignored it. Tapped the wheel with her thumbnail, thinking. If this was Cortez, or one of his new playmates, they were being smart. Not pushing. Just watching. That was worse. She'd almost prefer the reckless drive-by, the quick and sometimes unthinkable violence Houston did best. At least then you could see them coming.

Genevieve considered pulling over, walking into a gas station to see if the driver would follow her inside, but something told her not to break her pattern. If she looked scared, they'd smell blood. Instead, she took the next right, a turn she never made on her usual commute, then doubled back through a strip mall parking lot. The tail kept up, unwavering. Her hands never left the wheel as she threaded the car through narrow side streets, passing shuttered donut shops and the half-empty lots of payday loan stores. The city's morning haze was just lifting, and even in this hour the sun already burned through the windscreen, glare making it harder to see anything in the mirrors.

She studied the SUV, looking for markings. Rental plate. No stickers. A tiny dent by the passenger door, almost invisible unless you watched for it. She logged that in her mind. Noted that the windows were rolled up, no visible movement inside. Could be one person, could be three. Could be someone she'd never met, or someone who'd once sworn to protect her. In this business, loyalty was a coin that changed hands every time you blinked. Genevieve took another unexpected left, then a quick right onto a street under construction. The sedan behind her hesitated, but the SUV did not. They followed her through the maze of orange cones and blinking caution lights, always at a distance that felt both respectful and menacing.

Genevieve felt her pulse surge. She was angry now, not frightened. It was elemental and volcanic, the kind that built up in her chest and never left. She thought of calling Renny, but she didn't want to send him on a rampage—not yet, not unless things escalated beyond surveillance. She knew how he'd react: full heat, no subtlety, burn the whole city if it kept her safe. She didn't want that. Not yet.

She dialed her personal assistant Sam instead, Bluetooth voice activation, eyes never leaving the mirror.

"Good morning, Mrs. O'Neal," Sam answered, alert.

"Someone's following me," Genevieve said, voice flat. "Silver SUV. Tinted. Possible rental. Get security to sweep the garage before I arrive. And text me when you see it enter the lot."

Sam was already vigilant. "You want back-up?"

"No. Just eyes."

She ended the call. The SUV dropped off for a moment, as if her voice alone could repel it, and then it reappeared, sliding into place as she merged onto the highway toward the office tower. For the next eleven minutes, it shadowed her. Never closer than two car lengths, never so far that she could forget it was there. Genevieve adjusted her seat and cranked the AC. She could outlast anyone in a staring contest, even if it happened through a mirror at seventy miles an hour.

Near downtown, she executed a final maneuver—took the express exit for the convention center, then circled back through the labyrinth of one-way streets. She lost sight of the SUV twice, once behind a city bus and once behind a taxi, but both times it reemerged, persistent as a nightmare. She almost smiled. They wanted her to see them, but not enough to make a scene. Amateurs, she thought. Or else someone sending her a warning: We can reach you, even here. She pulled into her building's underground lot, lights flickering overhead, concrete still damp from last night's rain. She didn't see the SUV but assumed it was lurking on one of the upper floors, watching her from some dark alcove. She parked in her reserved spot, shut off the engine, and sat for a long beat. The world was still. Even her hands were steady as she reached for her purse and checked the .38 revolver inside—a ritual, but a comfort.

She smoothed her hair, reapplied lipstick, and stepped out into the echoing silence of the garage. Her heels rang out with each step, sharp and unyielding. She didn't hurry. She wanted them to see her, wanted them to know she wasn't afraid. When she reached the elevator, Sam was waiting just inside the doors, eyes scanning the garage behind her.

"See anything?" Genevieve asked, voice low.

"Nothing yet, but I got security looking at the guest log. If they come inside, we'll know." Sam handed her a coffee, black and bitter.

"Keep watching. If they're good, we don't want them to know we're onto them."

They rode the elevator together in silence, the city bleeding through the glass windows as they ascended. Only when they stepped onto the twenty-fourth floor—her domain, the epicenter of the empire she'd built with blood and brilliance—did Genevieve allow herself to breathe. She walked in with her head high, heels clicking out the same message as always: Fuck around and find out if you want.

Just as Genevieve began to relax and forget her stressful morning, a knock interrupted her peace. Sam was outside the frosted glass wall of her corner office, double checking the appointment schedule again. After the tense morning, he was aware any unexpected visitor would be unwelcome. His heart raced, and the faint taste of fear was on his tongue.

"Uh, Mrs. O'Neal... He hesitated, knowing she hated the surname, always preferring just "Ms." or "Boss." "You have a visitor. Not on the schedule."

Genevieve raised a brow. "Unannounced?"

The assistant nodded, clearly rattled. "She said you'd know who she is."

Genevieve's mind spun through the potential unwanted possibilities. Renny's mistress? A creditor? Worse—a regulator? But the off-script confidence in Sam's voice said neither. She waved a hand, "Send her in, and bring me another coffee. Black."

Sam retreated, and a moment later the glass door opened again. Light fractured on the beveled "O'Neal Group" logo as the woman glided through, heels clicking a lazy, unhurried tempo on the Italian marble. The effect was deliberate, staged for maximum intimidation.

She was five-eight in four-inch pumps, bone-straight hair in a sharp center part, features feminine—cheekbones like blades, eyes smoky quartz. Her skin was caramel, unblemished; her lashes thick, lips lacquered, the line of her jaw uncompromising. The designer clutch—cream dress, fit like a bespoke glove. The only jewelry was diamond studs, a platinum watch and a massive emerald cut diamond wedding ring. Sophistication and danger braided together in one look.

Genevieve didn't rise. She stared, weighing the threat. The woman smiled, a flare of white teeth but it wasn't soft. "Damn," Genevieve finally murmured, and then she stood up, pushing back her white leather chair. "The legendary Precious

Cummings. In the flesh. What brings you all the way to Houston? Although I'm thrilled to see you, his can't be a good sign."

Precious gave a slow clap, then set her purse on the desk "Genevieve O'Neal, I'm thrilled to see you too baby girl," she replied, voice silk wrapped around steel, "before we get to business, give me a hug," her tone half-greeting, half-warning.

Genevieve moved around the desk and embraced her tightly. "It's been too long."

"Too long and too quiet," Precious replied. "Which is exactly why I'm here."

Genevieve studied her. "Genesis sent you, didn't he?"

Precious nodded. "Said you were in the middle of a storm but still trying to act like it's not raining."

Genevieve exhaled, sinking back into her chair. "What did he find?"

"Enough," Precious said. "His people did a deep dive on that girl Shay Whitaker. Background's a lie, work history's patched, and she's been using a ghost line tied to Cortez Mercer."

Genevieve's eyes narrowed. "I knew it. I been watching her." She gestured to Sam, who entered with two coffees, then retreated wordlessly.

Precious pressed her almond shaped French manicured nails together. "You always did keep nice staff." She took a long sip, then set the cup down, eyes never leaving Genevieve's face. "But nice can also mean naive, which is why I came in person. Genesis is worried about you."

Genevieve bristled. "I can take care of myself. I grew up with wolves." She smiled tightly. "And you know I got sharp teeth."

"I do." Precious scanned the office—spare, elegant, expensive. "Look at what you've accomplished. You went from modeling to having all this. We're all proud of you. You're like the little sister I wish I had," she said returning the smile. "But this Shay girl is up to no good and Genesis sent me to shut the shit down. He would've come personally, but he is dealing with a very serious issue in New York."

Genevieve frowned. "I knew his situation was much more dire than he was letting on"

"It is but your brother, Supreme and Nico are handling it. Our concern is you. We need to make a move," Precious said. "Genesis didn't like what he saw. He said Shay ain't just some pawn—she's embedded. She is reporting to Cortez directly. And we know that Cortez is in business with Maverick. Maverick is the face up front but Cortez is in deep just low key in the back, but equally as dangerous."

Genevieve clenched her jaw. "That means you all think I'm a target."

Precious leaned forward, voice low and direct. "We know you're a target. And Genesis said if anything happens to you, he's burning Houston down, and we don't want that," Precious smiled.

Genevieve was silent for a moment, then sighed. "Shay is definitely suspect but are you positive she is aligned with Cortez?"

"More than positive. Genesis found direct proof. Besides her background, college transcripts, all fabricated, she's been using a ghost number to check in every morning." Precious paused, letting it land.

Genevieve braced. "Who's on the other end of that line?"

Precious's smile was small and grim. "Cortez Mercer."

A slow breath. Genevieve bit down on her lip. "Fuck. This is problematic."

"That's why I'm here," Precious replied. "And it gets worse. The line cross-checks to a burner owned by Maverick's crew out of Atlanta. These people are playing chess, not checkers."

Genevieve thought about that for a long, narrow moment. Her fingers curled into fists, then released. "And here I was worried about Brice and his relationship with Pilar, when Shay is the real threat," she shook her head. "What do you suggest?"

Precious adjusted her position in the chair, first uncrossing then recrossing her legs, and leaned forward. "Shay is more than a mole. She's deep into it. Watching you, reporting every meeting, every move. She's figured out your routine, and they might have someone following you."

Genevieve's nostrils flared, but her voice was measured. "I know they do. A silver SUV followed me to work this morning."

Precious tilted her head. "Do you think she could be working with anyone else within your staff? Someone close like Sam, maybe Pilar."

Genevieve shook her head. "Not Pilar. That girl is starting to feel like family to me."

"Even family talks. Especially when the threat is survival." Precious gripped her coffee. "I know you want to protect your people, but this isn't a game anymore. Cortez plays for keeps. Maverick, too."

Genevieve went to the window, gazed down at the city. "What do they want?"

"You," Precious said simply. "Alive, preferably. But dead if necessary. You hold a lot of power. You have personal close ties to both Renny and Genesis. You're also the only one who can hold the O'Neal operation together if Renny goes down. Which means if they take you out, the whole network goes soft."

Genevieve's voice was ice. "You're saying they'll come for me. Here."

"They're already here. Shay's just the advance team. I saw a black Escalade parked two levels below your reserved slot, with Georgia plates and no toll records. That's a holding pattern," Precious scoffed.

Genevieve shut her eyes, did the calculus. Every move, every meeting, every weakness. And then she opened them again, resolute. "What would you do if you were me?"

Precious smiled. It was the same wicked smile she'd worn as a teenager, when she started at the bottom from the projects of Brooklyn and rose to the top. Taking out anyone who stood in her way. "I'd cut the head off the snake. Quietly."

Genevieve laughed then, sudden and bright. "You're the best. That's why there's only one, Precious Cummings."

Precious grinned. "The feeling's mutual. But I need you to listen to me, Genevieve. They want to make a statement. We have to make our own first."

Genevieve went back to her desk, poured herself a shot of bourbon from the bottom drawer, and gave a second one to Precious. "So, we get ahead of it," she said. "We smoke out Shay and use her to trace the pipeline."

Precious considered. "She's dangerous, but not loyal. I can flip her. Give me forty-eight hours." She downed the bourbon and winced. "But once she's no longer of any use to us, then we smoke her."

Genevieve smiled, "You always did have a way with girls, so I'll let you deal with Shay for now."

Precious stood, smoothed her dress. "I'll be in touch. But keep a gun in your purse and your car." She checked her watch. "If Genesis calls, I'll tell him you got the message."

Genevieve nodded. "And tell him thanks for sending you."

Precious hesitated at the door, then looked back. "We know you're strong but you're not alone in this. Even if you want to be." Her eyes lingered. "We're family. We rise. We Fall. And get back up together."

The elevator dinged down the hall. Precious

slipped away, leaving only the faintest trace of perfume and gunpowder in her wake.

Genevieve sat for a while, silent, letting the tension coil and uncoil in her gut. Then she unlocked her phone, typed out a message to Pilar.

Be careful. Trust no one. If you see Shay, call me.

She hit send, then opened her desk drawer, checked the weight of the pistol inside, and closed it again.

A minute later Sam poked his head in. "Everything okay, Ms. O'Neal?"

She smiled, all teeth and no warmth. "Never better. And Sam, Precious is family. She is always welcomed here."

"Noted, boss," Sam nodded.

For the first time in months, Genevieve felt alive. If necessary, she was ready for war.

Brice was lacing up his running shoes when an unexpected knock broke his concentration. Strange—the doorman always called first. He checked his phone's door camera and recognized the visitor immediately.

"Shay?" he said, swinging the door open. "What are you doing here?"

"Not even a smile for me?" She slipped past him into the apartment, her perfume lingering in her wake.

"I was just heading out for a run, so make it quick."

"We play for the same team. I was expecting a little more hospitality." She surveyed his living room. "But anywho, Cortez mentioned that you whisked Pilar away for a weekend getaway. Progress report?"

"Pilar is handled. After our trip, I think I could get her to do anything I asked," he boasted.

"Even turn on Genevieve?"

"I said anything didn't I," Brice cracked.

Shay approached him, tracing a manicured nail along the contours of his biceps, trailing down his chest, hovering dangerously low near his dick print. "Your persuasive talents must be... impressive."

"They are," he replied, removing her hand with cool precision. "And now they're needed elsewhere. Stick to your assignment. I'll handle mine."

As Brice ushered her to the door, Shay couldn't decide if his dismissal annoyed or aroused her. Either way, she found herself wondering just how skilled he might be between the sheets.

The Walls Are Closing In

Chapter Fifteen

The sunlight in Pilar's apartment felt different that afternoon, filtered through the tears she hadn't yet let escape. She'd just stepped inside, waves of the weekend still clinging to her skin, the memory of Brice's hands mapping her body, his raw confessions, the way he said her name, that ache he left between her thighs and in her chest. The scarf he bought her still knotted in her curls, a silk tether to their brief, fevered escape. Her bag dropped by the door, she pressed her back against it, the hush of her apartment suddenly oppressive. She'd barely slept since the phone call, replaying every word, every omission. *She's all the way in.* That's what he'd said.

She wasn't sure what she was more hurt by—the lie, or the fact that it felt so good to believe it. She was in over her head—she knew it, and maybe that's why she couldn't stop. She felt bruised and alive, every nerve on its own tripwire.

Pilar peeled off her sandals and went to the kitchen, pouring herself a glass of water with hands that trembled just enough to spill a little on the counter. She stood there, breathing, remembering Brice's thumb tracing the hollow behind her ear, the taste of his mouth and the way his eyes went distant when she asked about his past. She told herself she didn't care. She told herself she was stronger than this, that she'd come up hard and learned to spot men who talked in riddles and ran game. But damn—it was so easy, so sweet, to believe even a beautiful lie.

She took her water to the window and scanned the street below. Cars idled, kids skateboarding in the lot, an old lady dragging her laundry cart. Nothing out of place. Except for the feeling chewing at her chest, the sense that she was already being watched, that the story was already writing itself, and she was just trying to read ahead.

Pilar was halfway through changing into a T-shirt and sweats when the knock came. Not a polite tap, not the buzzer—an actual knock. Three, even beats, then a pause, then two more. It made her freeze, water still in hand, shirt half-on. She set the glass down and tiptoed to the door, careful not to make the floorboards squeak. She peeked through the peephole and sighed with relief and frustration at once. It was Shay.

Shay, hair slicked back in a low bun, sun-glasses perched on her head. She wore skintight jeans and a white low-cut bodysuit, the kind that looked effortless but cost a grip. She had a bottle of wine in one hand and a brown grocery bag in the other, standing with one hip cocked, grinning like she was there to start trouble.

Pilar debated for a second—ignore, pretend not to be home, text her later with a lame excuse. But she could already feel Shay's energy seeping through the door, and she knew if she didn't answer, Shay would just up the pressure, maybe even call the landlord or knock on a neighbor's door. That's how she was. Persistent. Like a cat you never really owned.

Pilar cracked the door, just enough to show her face. "Hey..."

Shay's smile widened. "Hey boo! You dodging me, girl? I heard you was back in town but when you didn't answer my calls or text messages, I had to come make sure you didn't get snatched up by some fine-ass cartel prince down in Tulum."

"My phone's on do not disturb, so I haven't gotten any notifications," Pilar sighed, hoping Shay would take the hint she wanted to be left alone for the moment.

But instead, Shay held up the wine, then the bag. "I brought reinforcements. Thought we could catch up. We got some wine, and those little jalapeño crisps you like."

Pilar hesitated. She didn't want this. Not now. But refusing Shay might raise more red flags.

She opened the door wider. "Yeah. Cool. Come in."

Shay swept in, letting her gaze do a quick inventory of the place. "Damn. Somebody got their shit together since last time I was here. You Marie Kondo this bitch or just throw everything in the closet?" she joked.

She moved straight to the kitchen, popping the wine open one-handed and fishing two glasses from the drying rack. Pilar trailed behind, nerves prickling at the base of her neck.

"That vacation glow different."

Pilar forced a smile. "It was... chill."

They settled on the couch. Pilar took a sip of wine. Shay watched her intently.

"So," Shay said, dragging it out. "Brice... He the real deal or just another passport stamp?"

"What do you mean?" Pilar questioned.

Shay shrugged, took a crisp from the bag. "I mean, he got that whole mystery vibe. Quiet. Money. Fine as hell. But I don't really know much about him."

Pilar tilted her head. "You sure? Isn't he friends with the guy you know Trent?"

"Sure." Shay smirked. "But that don't mean I know Brice like that."

Pilar looked at her glass, then back at Shay. "Funny. You always seem to know just enough."

A flash of tension sparked in Shay's eyes—but she covered it fast, laughing like they were just swapping gossip.

"Nah, girl. I'm just nosy."

Pilar didn't laugh. She sipped her wine, not saying a word. Shay leaned back, changing the subject, talking about random things from work. But the air between them had shifted. It was thick now. Loaded.

"But on the real, I'm only asking you about Brice because I want you to be happy, and he seems to be doing that," Shay said, doing her best to sound genuinely concerned.

Pilar tried to play nonchalant, shrugging as she sipped wine. "He's cool. It was just a weekend getaway. No big deal."

Shay wouldn't let up, pushing for details. "That's not what your IG said. You went full 'future wifey' mode with those sunrises and motivational quotes."

Pilar rolled her eyes, not in the mood to deal with Shay's mouth and intrusive questions. Pilar set her wine glass down, fingers drumming the rim. "Why you really here, Shay?"

The question hung there, echoing a little too loud in the quiet apartment.

Shay shrugged, feigning innocence. "Can't a girl check on her friend?"

They both knew better. Shay didn't do random pop-ins. Shay didn't do concern that wasn't mixed with curiosity, or, more accurately, agenda.

"Well, you've checked up on me and I'm fine," Pilar lied. She glanced inside the bag, taking a few jalapeño crisps and dipping them in some fancy cheese. Shay watched her closely, as if every bite revealed a page of her diary.

They continued to sit on the couch, legs curled, sunlight dappling the floor. Shay peppered her with small talk about work, distant friends, gossip from her old neighborhood. But every so often, she circled back to Brice making the tension linger.

Shay's eyes kept flicking to her phone, the grocery bag, the apartment. She was gathering intel, and Pilar knew it. At one point, Shay excused herself to the bathroom, and Pilar caught herself scanning Shay's phone screen, which was left unlocked and face-up on the coffee table. A string of recent texts: Unknown Numbers, abbreviations, a couple of times Pilar's own name. Her stomach twisted. When Shay came back, Pilar decided to test her. She let her guard down, or pretended to, leaning in close and lowering her voice. "Can I tell you something?"

Shay's eyes widened, hungry. "Always."

Pilar hesitated, then said, "I think I'm falling for Brice, but I'm scared. I don't want to fuck it up."

Shay nodded, sympathetic, but Pilar saw the flash of calculation behind it.

"Just be careful," Shay said. "I'm here for you,

always. You know that, right? You can tell me anything."

Pilar smiled but felt the ice down her spine. Because now, she knew—Shay wasn't just asking questions. She was collecting intel. And if Brice was lying…Shay might already know more than she was saying.

They lingered there a while, the sun crawling across the floor, conversation looping back on itself. Shay eventually stood, gathering her things, and gave Pilar a quick, tight hug. Her lips brushed Pilar's cheek.

"Call me if ever need to talk or just want to hang out. I'm always here for you," Shay's voice so sweet, Pilar knew it had to be poison.

They exchanged fake kisses, and Pilar was happy to walk Shay to the door and watch her leave, suspecting she might be an enemy.

Genevieve hadn't slept. She'd sat up reading every word of every report brought to her by her privately paid-for security team, every flagged irregularity in the building's overnight logs, every blurry still of a car that might or might not have tailed her from the gated community to her office tower. She'd even reviewed Sam's call log, not because she doubted her assistant, but because trust—real trust—was a luxury she'd forfeited long ago.

Now, at 9:07 a.m., she perched at the edge of her glass-topped desk in a ribbed cashmere dress the color of wet sand, not bothering with her usual armor of heels, all the better to haul ass if it came to that. Her eyes were red-rimmed from exhaustion and caffeine, and the only illumination in the room was the blue glow of the split-screen security monitor. Genevieve watched herself on one, watched the elevator bank on the other. She was about to take another sip of her espresso when Sam notified her Pilar was here.

"Send her in," Genevieve said without looking up.

An eternity passed in the time it took for Pilar to cross the lobby, ride the elevator, and appear in the frosted glass doorway. She looked like a contradiction incarnate: hair smoothed into a perfect top knot that only accentuated the uneven flush of her cheekbones and the dark circles under her eyes, a long cardigan thrown over the clothes she'd clearly slept in, oversized sunglasses hiding the war in her gaze. She barely acknowledged Sam as he opened the door and closed it behind her in one soft click.

Genevieve stayed seated, her eyes locked on Pilar, studying every micro-expression with the intensity of a scientist examining a new specimen. "You alright?" she asked, voice so gentle it almost didn't belong to her.

Pilar stood in the center of the room, uncertain, then unwrapped her scarf and slid the sunglasses off. Her eyes were puffy, red, not from crying but from whatever kept her up all night. She hesitated before speaking, the way you do when the words you're about to say will change the world, or at least your place in it.

"I need to talk to you, it's important," Pilar said, voice smaller than usual.

Genevieve gestured to the slate-blue guest chair opposite her. "Sit. You want coffee?"

Pilar shook her head, so Genevieve reached for her own espresso, sipped, then set it down without tasting. The silence stretched as Pilar looked out at the city through the floor-to-ceiling windows, as if she could find a good reason not to do what she had come to do. She sat, smoothing her hands over the cheap polyester of her joggers.

"Is this about the text I sent, telling you to be

careful and to call me if you see Shay?" Genevieve asked, her tone warm, attempting to find a way through Pilar's defenses.

Pilar's lips barely moved. "Yes and no. I apologize for not responding yesterday but I had my phone on do not disturb. I just read your text this morning. I did see Shay. She came by my apartment yesterday. But this isn't about her."

Pilar's hands shook under the desk, so she pressed her knees together and anchored herself in the chair. "I heard Brice on the phone the last night we were on our trip... after we... after everything. He didn't know I was awake." She glanced at Genevieve, trying to gauge whether this was about to become an inquisition.

Genevieve watched her with the same impassive stare she used to unnerve junior partners in board meetings. "What did he say?"

It took Pilar two tries before she could get the words out. "He mentioned your name. Said I didn't suspect anything. Said he was playing it soft. He mentioned Cortez. And Mav." Her voice cracked on the last name.

Genevieve's expression didn't change, but something in her posture did. She straightened up, tilting her head in a way that, if you knew her, meant she was preparing to obliterate the enemy. "He has no idea you overheard him?"

Pilar shook her head, eyes shining with humiliation and anger. "No, I completely played it off although I wanted to cry, kill him and vomit all at the same time."

Genevieve stood and began pacing behind her desk, high and slow, the way a caged animal does before it remembers it can bite. The name Cortez was a trigger for her. "Trust me I understand. Betrayal is a knife you only feel after it's already inside you," she said, not looking at Pilar yet. Her voice was almost clinical, as if she needed the distance to say what had to be said. "This sort of a betrayal from a man you love is devastating."

Pilar wiped at her eyes, refusing to let the tears fall. "It's not just that," she whispered. "I feel stupid. I thought he really—" She broke off, shaking her head.

Genevieve finally looked her in the eye, and for a moment all the steely control fell away. She gently placed her hand on Pilar's shoulder. "You're not stupid. You're human. You wanted to believe. That's what they count on."

Pilar nodded, but the shame lingered. The silence stretched, and in it was every unspoken thing: the fact that they were both, in the end, alone. That no matter the money, the connections, the alliances—they were drawing lines on a battlefield where the rules changed every hour.

"This stays between us for now," Genevieve said, voice back to steel. "Since Brice is working for them, we need to flip the script. You think you can keep playing your part?"

Pilar's eyes widened. "You want me to keep pretending?"

Genevieve met her gaze, all pretense stripped away. "I want you to survive. If you can stomach it, I'll get you out when it's time."

Pilar sat back, trying to imagine what it would feel like to play Brice the way he'd played her. To meet his eyes and not flinch. She realized that this was exactly what Genevieve needed from her—not just loyalty, but for her to be tougher. "I can do it," she said, forcing the words out. "I'll do whatever you need."

Genevieve's fingers tightened on her shoulder for a moment, then released. "Good. Because things are about to get messy."

Pilar rode the elevator down in a haze, watching the numbers descend and wondering what her face looked like to the camera in the corner. Had she hidden the fear? Had she betrayed herself, or was she about to?

Pilar walked out and into the parking structure. As she reached her car, her phone buzzed—a message from Brice.

I miss you. Can't wait to be with you again.

She stared at the words. She imagined herself replying, imagined herself throwing the phone into traffic, imagined herself showing up at his door with a gun and a smile and a story about a woman scorned. Instead, she put the phone away and slid into her seat, letting her body fold into the contours of the leather and her mind flatten into blankness. Pilar knew she couldn't be weak. Genevieve needed a soldier.

Takedown

Chapter Sixteen

Shay didn't know it yet, but her time was up. She left her go-to café in River Oaks, phone in hand, thumb moving fast across the encrypted chat app, caffeinated blood humming through her veins. It was the hour when the city seemed to lean forward, all its people in a hurry to get somewhere else. Shay was halfway to her car, eyes on a distant point, when the black SUV—sitting curbside, engine idling—came to life and ghosted forward. There was no screech of tires, no suddenness, just a smooth mechanical inevitability. Before she could even register the move, the back door eased open, and the interior yawned at her like the mouth of a cave.

She hesitated, but only for a second. There was a presence behind her. A shadow that suggested speed, hunger, and a willingness to do whatever it took. She spun, ready to bolt, but a hand—strong and cool—clamped onto her arm and pulled her in.

Inside, the air smelled of leather, cologne, and something harsh, like ozone or fear. The SUV's back seat was already occupied. Shay was faced with a woman that appeared dangerous but gorgeous at the same time, it was eerie. Hair so smooth it was like a blade, eyes darker than obsidian.

"My name is Precious, and I've been looking for you."

"Precious Cummings..." Shay uttered. The woman's name had a mythos in Shay's world, but she'd never met her in person. Now she was faced with a presence that didn't so much fill the space as command it. Genevieve had once joked that Precious had been grown in a lab to make other women nervous. Shay understood that now, viscerally.

Precious didn't smile. "Yes, but that's my

maiden name. I'm sure you know I'm married to Supreme. But we're not here to discuss me. I came for you," she said, her voice low and perfectly enunciated. The words left her mouth with the finality of a death sentence. Death on the tongue, Genevieve would have said.

Shay tried to wrench away. "Who the fuck—" But the grip on her arm just tightened. Shay peered up and recognized Dre, the enforcer, his face a mask of complete indifference. Dre wore all black and had a way of moving that made him look like he could materialize out of any shadow in the city. His eyes barely flicked in her direction as he propelled her further inside. The door slammed shut behind her, the sound final as a gunshot.

Midas was driving. She could see his eyes in the rearview, two green points of light, always tracking, always calculating. Shay's first instinct was to fight. She reached for her purse, but it was already gone. Dre must have stripped it off her mid-motion. She went for her phone. Nothing but flat palms and empty pockets. She glanced at the window, calculated the probabilities of kicking it out before Dre snapped her neck. The odds weren't in her favor. Instead, she set her jaw and glared at Precious.

"Let me out," Shay growled, voice trembling. "I don't know what you've heard, but—"

Precious cut her off, words as sharp as broken glass. "What I heard is irrelevant. What matters is what you did, and who you did it for."

Shay tried to play it cool, but her heart was a bird, slamming itself against bone. "This is a misunderstanding," she managed. "I work for Genevieve. If there's some beef, we can talk it out like..."

Dre twisted in his seat so fast it made her jerk back instinctively. "You don't work for her," he said. "You work for Cortez and Maverick. Or maybe you're just freelancing, but either way, you been running your mouth in all the wrong places."

There was a silence, the SUV was moving fast now, out of the commercial district, taking sharp turns, doubling back. Shay knew the route. They weren't headed anywhere public.

"You gonna kill me?" she asked, and her voice was almost steady.

Precious took a compact mirror out of her purse and checked her lipstick, as if this was all a minor inconvenience. "Not if you cooperate," she said. "But if you want to do this the uncomfortable way, I promise you—simply killing you, would be showing compassion."

They drove for what felt like an hour but was probably twenty minutes. When the SUV finally slowed, Shay made a mental note of the darkened streets, the abandoned building, the lack of witnesses. She was already cataloguing details for her own future statement to the police, but right now her lungs were refusing to fill all the way. Midas killed the engine.

Precious stepped out first, heels clicking like a countdown. "Bring her."

Dre didn't give Shay time to protest. He popped the door open and dragged her by the elbow, not rough—but firm enough to remind her that options had expired. Inside the place looked gutted. Graffiti on the walls, old bleachers broken in half, chain nets still swaying on hoops that hadn't seen a ball in years. A single hanging bulb swung over the center of the room like a noose made of light.

Midas pulled out a metal folding chair and slammed it down. "Sit."

Shay stayed standing.

"I said sit." His tone cut like steel.

She sat. There were folding chairs set up in a circle, like this was going to be an AA meeting. Once seated, Dre zip-tied her wrists behind her back. He checked the bonds with an efficiency that suggested he'd done this a thousand times. Precious leaned against a support beam, arms crossed, one stiletto heel tapping out a patient rhythm.

Shay tried to center herself. She remembered advice from an old mentor: If you're going to die, do it with dignity. She looked Dre in the eye. "So, what, you gonna beat a confession out of me?"

Dre didn't answer, just stood back and let Precious take the lead. The silence stretched. Shay felt the pulse in her neck, the dryness in her mouth. Precious regarded her for a long time, then finally spoke.

"You're going to tell me everything Cortez asked you to do, what he knows and what is the endgame."

Shay's mouth went dry. "I never—" she began, but Dre's hand snapped out and caught her across the face, open palm, a warning more than a punishment.

"Don't lie," Precious said calmly. "You know the second time I ask; it gets worse."

Shay's mind flickered through her options. She could stall. She could tell half-truths. But judging from the look in Precious' eyes, she would sniff out her bullshit. If she told them the truth, she'd be dead. If she didn't, she'd be dead slower.

She looked from Precious to Dre, then thought about Midas who was still waiting in the car. The world seemed to shrink down to just this room, just this moment, just this choice.

"You gonna let me talk?" Shay spat blood onto the floor and forced herself to smirk. "Or you just want a punching bag?"

Dre glanced at Precious. She gave a slight nod. Dre stepped back.

"Start talking," Precious said, voice flat as a scalpel.

Shay started with the truth and mixed in just enough fiction to try to save herself. She told them about the phone calls from Cortez, about the burner phones, about the drop spot in the park where she left envelopes for pickup. She told them about the night she bugged Pilar's phone, about the time Genevieve was followed by a car that wasn't from their crew. She phrased it all in a way that made her look like a victim, like she'd been forced into it, like she was just trying to survive.

Precious listened, nodded. At one point, she pulled out her own phone and started scrolling through texts, cross-referencing names and dates.

As Shay reached the end of her story, she realized she was trembling. Her hands hurt from the zipties. There was a metallic taste in her mouth.

"I've told you everything," Shay finished. "You can check my phone. I got nothing left."

Dre stepped forward and unlocked her phone with a thumbprint he'd lifted while restraining her. He handed it to Precious, who scrolled methodically, screen reflecting cold blue light onto her face. She read for a long time, then set the phone down.

"You left out the asset in Brice's building," Precious said quietly. "You wanna tell me about that?"

Shay's heart crumpled. She'd forgotten about the janitor; the one Cortez had bribed months ago. Her last hope was gone. She sagged in the chair and let out a ragged breath.

"Okay," she whispered. "I'll tell you."

Precious moved so quickly that Shay barely had time to wince. She crouched down in front of her, ten inches away, and stared straight into Shay's soul.

"You're gonna die," Precious said softly, her tone calm and unwavering. "It can be quick, or it can be painfully drawn out. Don't force me to choose your outcome."

Shay nodded, her eyes wide with fear. In that moment, she was no longer the woman she had become—she was a six-year-old girl again, terrified of the boogeyman, not ready to die. How had it come to this? And was it too late to rewrite her fate? She began spilling all the tea. Everything about the building, about Brice's patterns, about the night access. All she could remember, desperate to prove her value. When she finished, Dre cut her wrists loose with a pocketknife. She sagged forward, not sure if she was about to be shot or dumped back on the street.

Precious straightened, brushing the dust from her knees, and looked down at Shay with the cold gaze of a disappointed mother.

"You've bought yourself a few more hours to live," she said flatly, then turned to Dre. "Keep an eye on her. I'll be back."

Chapter Seventeen

Cortez stood at the window of a penthouse suite, twenty-eight floors up, He ran a hand over his jaw, feeling the rough stubble while staring through the tinted glass, at the city of Houston below, laid out like a chessboard soaked in gasoline. It was crooked, chaotic and full of secrets. The whole place breathed like a wounded animal, chewing its own leg off just to survive. Cortez respected that. He lived for that. He was that.

He unlocked his phone with a thumbprint. Shay's name sat at the top of the thread, glowing green, unread. He didn't bother calling her back. She was compromised—wrung out, tapped, just like everybody else who thought pressure was a myth until it crushed their lungs. He scrolled down, past dead drop numbers and encrypted threats, until he hit the one name that mattered: Maverick. He hit CALL. Three rings.

"Talk to me." Even over a secure line, Maverick's voice was smooth but razor-sharp—like velvet over barbed wire.

"Shay's done," Cortez said, no warm-up. "Vernon tracked her to a parking lot in River Oaks. She got scooped about two hours ago. Clean grab. No struggle, no cameras. Intel points to Precious."

He let the name hang like smoke. Maverick didn't react. Just that signature pause—the kind that meant he was already doing the math in his head.

"You got confirmation?"

"I got enough," Cortez said. "Shay's phone went dark the second Dre's burner pinged two blocks over. Then I get a box of cigars left at the Fifth Ward stash spot—with a note that said, 'Next time, it's your lungs.' That's Renny."

Maverick chuckled low. "Nigga got style. I'll give him that."

Cortez didn't crack a smile. "You wanna tell

me why we're getting hit from three sides? If there's something you holding back, now's the time to spit it out."

More silence. Then Maverick came in with more authority. "Word is another crew's trying to wedge in. Things are shifting. We need leverage. It's time we snatch up Genevieve."

Cortez eyes narrowed. "That's a tough grab. She's got ex-military personnel watching her, Tripwires on top of cameras and stealth surveillance. She's paranoid, but smart. We touch her, it'll be war."

"Then we don't touch her directly," Maverick said. "We touch somebody she cares about. Somebody soft. Somebody she'll walk into the fire for."

Cortez turned from the window, pacing. A half-played chessboard sat on a glass table— queen frozen mid-threat. He tapped a rook with his thumb, thinking.

"Pilar," he said.

"Exactly," Maverick replied. "She ain't built for this. She folds, Genevieve bleeds."

Cortez's phone buzzed. He glanced down. PING: ***Pilar—Montrose. Solo.***

A slow grin crept onto his face. "She's at a bar in Montrose. Alone. Or so she thinks," Cortez said.

"Send Vernon," Maverick said. "And tell that fool not to fuck this up."

Cortez ended the call with no goodbye. He walked over to the bar cart, poured two fingers of Yamazaki, and stared back out at the city. He drank it slow, the burn in his chest grounding him.

Then he sent the orders: ***Grab Pilar. Bring her to the West Loop safehouse. No bruises above the neck. Break a few fingers if she fights. But keep her clean.***

Cortez was a pro. He liked precision. He liked control.

He pulled up the security feed on his tablet. A black SUV slid into an alley behind the Montrose bar. Vernon and two hitters jumped out—hoods up, masks tight. Pilar stumbled out the back, tipsy, phone in hand. She didn't even scream. She just vanished.

He watched it all play out like a scene he'd storyboarded himself. He made a note to dock Vernon's pay if she came back with bruises. He poured another drink and moved the white queen on the board. Check. Genevieve wouldn't ignore this one. She'd come to him. And when she did, he'd be ready. He got up from the table, closed the curtains, and let the city vanish behind a layer of midnight and glass.

Pilar's scream never made it out of her throat. There was the faintest intake of breath, a nascent noise in her chest, and then the world folded. Arms around her midsection lifted her body off the sidewalk, jamming the air from her lungs with a practiced squeeze. One of the hands, rough and deliberate, clamped over her jaw, thumb digging into the hinge just below her ear, cutting off sound and thought at the same time. Her heels scuffed the pavement and then—nothing, only dark, a lurching pressure, the sour reek of spilled vodka and rubber. Somewhere behind her, the neon haze of the Montrose bar blinked oblivious encouragement to the street, but the reality of it receded as the back door of the SUV slammed shut.

The interior was black leather, cold and unsentimental. No windows in back. Pilar blinked, eyes struggling to adjust, mind racing to catalog what had just happened. She tried to twist, but someone else was already there, pinning her shoulders with the measured pressure of a man who didn't need to prove anything. Up front, a silhouette hissed: "Don't scream. You'll make it worse." The words were steady, almost kind, and utterly final.

They pulled away from the curb, the engine's growl swelling and then evening out as they merged with the city's arterial. Pilar's mind absorbed her surroundings in a single sweep. Three men. The one who'd grabbed her—heavy, probably a linebacker in high school, his breath hot with menthols and Red Bull, hands meaty enough to break fingers by accident. His partner, riding shotgun, glanced back only once but his gaze was clinical; he'd done this before, maybe a dozen times, maybe a hundred. The driver hummed tunelessly, his rhythm matching the turn signals, exuding the bored concentration of a man running an errand.

No one said her name. No one said anything. It was as if her existence was a technicality, a package to be delivered, no more meaningful than a bulk shipment of lithium batteries. But Pilar wasn't the same girl who used to count tips and chase after compliments. She'd seen too much. Heard too much. Her world had hardened around the harsh truth: people would do anything if you gave them the right excuse and the perfect alibi.

And in the quiet hum of that ride, she didn't cry, she didn't panic, she didn't beg. She studied. In the pulsing dark, Pilar listened. Every sound told a story—the backfire of the engine, the click of a magazine as someone checked a pistol, the urgent rustle of nylon as the men adjusted their jackets and their nerves. The two in back wore cheap sneakers, soles worn slick, probably didn't have a second pair. The driver wore cologne—something synthetic, a sharp citrus mated with chemical musk, the kind of scent that wanted so badly to be expensive it gave itself away. She could work with that.

Pilar waited for her captors to relax, to show their tells. The big one's knee jiggled whenever the SUV stopped at a light; he hated the inactivity, needed constant forward motion. The one pinning her kept his hand on her shoulder but drifted, distracted, to his phone every few minutes, thumb tapping out nervous little messages. The driver, for all his apparent detachment, watched her in the rearview, eyes flickering with curiosity or contempt; she could not yet tell which.

The city outside was familiar, but the route wasn't. They took an exit Pilar didn't recognize, sweeping down into a tangle of overpasses and half-lit service roads. She counted time, the distance between turns, the subtle change in air pressure as they went from highway to surface street. In another life, she might have let herself cry. But in this one, she memorized every curve and bump, every landmark in the dark, storing it away for when—or if—she needed to escape.

At last, the SUV jerked to a stop. She heard a gate roll open, the scrape of metal on metal, then the crunch of gravel under tires. There was a brief, murmured conference up front. No one touched her again until the doors unlocked with a soft, unanimous click. The linebacker reached over and, once more, pressed fingers into her arm—not cruelly, but with the confidence of a man who knew how to relocate joints if required.

"Get out," he said, to the point.

She complied, chin up, heels scraping down onto the gravel. The air outside was colder than she'd expected, raw and chemical, like a freezer full of bleach. Floodlights blazed to life. They were in a loading dock behind some kind of warehouse, iron bars and bare cinderblock as far as the eye could see. Her brain instantly mapped it: one way in, one way out, dozens of places to stash a body.

They hustled her inside, one hand on her elbow, the other always ready just behind her neck.

The hallway was narrow, ugly, and the overhead fluorescents buzzed with insectile energy. She was steered through a labyrinth of bare offices, past a vending machine, past a kitchenette reeking of burnt coffee and ancient tuna.

Finally, they ushered her into a room that was not a room—it was more of a cage, really, with a folding chair and a wobbly card table and a ring of security cameras mounted in every corner. A single light bulb hung from an extension cord, swaying slightly as if in anticipation.

The men deposited her in the chair and stood back. For the first time, Pilar could see their faces clearly. The big one's nose had been broken at least twice; his eyes were small and pale, but not unkind. The other wore a windbreaker and had the hunched posture of someone always expecting to be disappointed. The driver remained outside, chain-smoking, his silhouette drifting back and forth past the glass.

She waited for the questions, the threats, the script she'd been rehearsing since childhood. Instead, they just looked at her, appraising. For a tense, charged moment, everyone remained silent. Then, finally, the big one reached into his jacket and pulled out a battered notebook, flipped it open, and said: "You know why you're here?"

Pilar nodded, steady as ever. "Because I can get to Genevieve," she said, voice flat but proud. "And you need her more than you need me."

The men exchanged a glance—not surprise, but something closer to respect.

The one with the notebook grinned, a little wolfish. "Then let's start, shall we?"

Genevieve's morning started like a test she hadn't studied for. Her silk blouse was pristine, hair tucked in a loose chignon, but the muscle twitching in her neck whispered that something was off. At first, she blamed the usual culprits—tenant drama, vendor delays, another contract gone sideways. But the second she stepped out the front door of the new River Oaks rental, her latest, shiniest acquisition, her instincts were on fire. It wasn't the Houston heat, or the low hum of traffic echoing off the gated brick walls. It was the stillness. The kind that made you feel watched.

The first red flag: a blacked-out sedan parked two houses down. Not a rideshare, not private security. Just sitting there—engine cold, windows tinted. She couldn't see inside, but the reflection staring back from the windshield—hers—looked like a woman being scoped. She didn't freeze. Instead, she raised her phone as if she was answering a call and snapped three photos: the plates, the curb, the sedan. Then she walked to her car, calm and poised, but her eyes never left that driver's side window.

For a second, she swore she saw a silhouette shift—just the brim of a hat tilting. Watching. Genevieve got in, locked her doors, and pulled off. The sedan didn't follow. But the chill in her bones rode shotgun all the way downtown.

By the time she reached her office, her nerves were strung tight. She had one foot inside the lobby when her phone lit up—no contact, just numbers. Normally, she'd send it to voicemail.

Today, she answered.

"Genevieve O'Neal?" the voice was male. Rough, like concrete dragging across asphalt.

"Who wants to know?" Her tone was crisp. Controlled.

Static. Then a struggle—shuffling, grunting, like someone trying to grab the phone. Then a panicked voice broke through. High. Female. Desperate.

"Genevieve—don't—don't come. Whatever they say, don't—!"

It was Pilar. The phone was snatched back. A thud. A muffled groan. Then the first man again.

"You want to see your friend alive, do what I say. I'll text the address. Sixty minutes. Come alone. Try anything slick, and we'll start mailing pieces of her back."

The call ended. Genevieve stared at her screen, her own reflection flickering in the black glass. Her body moved on autopilot, heart thumping like war drums. A text dropped seconds later: a location. Warehouse address. Local number. She didn't flinch. She turned to leave, snatching her bag, already formulating a response plan. But her assistant, Sam, stepped in her path.

"Mrs. O'Neal, there's someone here to see you. Says it's urgent."

Genevieve frowned. "Who is it?"

Sam stepped aside, and in walked Precious—all bone-white pantsuit and diamond hoops, lips painted in a shade of red that looked more like a warning than a fashion statement.

"Close the door," Precious said, her voice flat as a propeller.

Genevieve obeyed. For once, she didn't try to run the room.

"They took Pilar," she said, swallowing hard. "I just got the call. She told me not to come, but—"

She stopped, breath hitching. Crying was no longer in her nature. But this… this was different.

Precious said nothing for a moment. She walked to the window, scanned the skyline, then sighed. It seemed she'd just heard some annoying news, not a potential death sentence.

"Who's they?"

"A man. Sounded like gravel and bad intentions. But I know it's Cortez's crew."

Precious nodded once, connecting the dots. "What do they want?"

"They said to come alone." Genevieve's voice cracked, just barely. "They sent me an address."

"You're not going," Precious said, matter-of-fact.

Genevieve stiffened. "You don't get to tell me—"

"I do when walking into that trap gets both of you killed," Precious said, cutting her off. She spun to face Genevieve with cold fire in her eyes. "That's not a demand. That's bait. You go in solo; you don't come out. Neither does she."

Genevieve inhaled through her nose, sharp and shaky. "I have to do something. I'm not about to sit here and watch Pilar get slaughtered."

"You're not sitting," Precious replied. "You're listening to me. This isn't about ransom. They want something else—leverage, control. You walk into that alone, it's checkmate."

Genevieve's hands curled into fists. "Then what do we do?"

"First, you forward me that address. Second, you call your security firm. I want eyes on this building immediately. No muscle—surveillance only. Nobody moves unless I say so."

Genevieve obeyed. She sent the address, then called in reinforcements. When she hung up, Precious was already texting, then dialing. The call lasted all of thirty seconds. When she turned back, her tone changed.

"You listen to me. Right now, you are the most valuable piece on the board. And the only reason Pilar's still breathing is because they think you'll crack. Stay in this office. Don't answer unknown numbers. Don't go anywhere alone. And don't play hero."

Genevieve sat on the edge of the couch, body still, but inside she was a riot. "If they hurt her—"

"If they hurt her, we burn every motherfucker involved to ash," Precious said, her voice icy enough to frost glass. "But not until I say so."

Just then, another call buzzed. Private number. Precious snatched the phone and answered without hesitation.

"You're speaking to Mrs. O'Neal's counsel. State your business."

The same raspy voice from before. "That's not what we agreed. She comes alone, or the bitch gets it."

Precious chuckled, the sound hollow and bone-dry. "Then tell your boss the deal's off. He gets both of us. Or nobody."

She hung up. Genevieve's phone buzzed again. A photo. Pilar—bruised, tied to a chair, eyes wild with fear.

Text: **Fifty minutes.**

Genevieve's hand trembled as she turned the screen to Precious. "He's not bluffing."

"No," Precious said. "He's not."

But her voice held no fear. Only fire. "Neither are we."

Not On My Watch

Chapter Eighteen

By noon, the house had transformed into a slow-burning furnace. The walls radiated heat, every surface filmed in greasy humidity, but Pilar didn't sweat. She sat in the center of the kitchen, wrists zip-tied behind the rungs of a scabbed oak chair, one ankle caulked to the leg with duct tape. The other foot tapped, measured, memorized. There were three men: the linebacker who called himself Vernon, the short baby faced one glued to his phone, and the third — rail-thin, nervous, the driver — who barely came inside. From where they'd left her, Pilar could see the entire first floor, open plan: the blue flicker of a TV on mute, empty pizza boxes, the dull shimmer of three pistols lined up on the counter.

She'd catalogued everything in the hour since they'd dumped her here. No windows but the greasy rectangle above the sink, front and back doors both bolted with hardware-store chains. She didn't care. The weakness was in the men. They worked in shifts. Vernon had clearly been in charge at first, pacing the room with the sidelong glare of a guy who'd watched too many gangster movies. But as the hours ticked on, his bravado began to leak. He checked his reflection every time he passed the fridge and flinched at the sound of his own phone vibrating. The baby-face kid barely looked at her, lost in his endless scrolling, and the third one kept vanishing into the backyard to smoke. None of them had bothered with masks. That told Pilar all she needed to know about their intentions.

She started with small things: coughing fits, dry heaving, pissing herself a little so the room would fill with the sharp, ammoniac stink. By the second hour, they'd stopped threatening her and started ignoring her. That was mistake number one. Although the pain in her hands was a constant throb every time she flexed, and the plastic ties would ground the nerves deeper, she kept at it.

She remembered, suddenly, the chicken factory in Bryan where she spent two weeks one summer, how the older women popped their knuckles in and out of joint so they could reach into the pulping machines when they jammed. Back then she'd tried it just for laughs, then puked when she heard the gristle pop. She practiced it now, counting under her breath, working the cartilage until the pinky snapped sideways and her palm went loose. A guttering scream escaped her — and in the next room, Vernon's footsteps went dead silent.

She let her head loll as he entered, face bent in concern that curdled instantly into disgust. "What the fuck is wrong with you?" he said, one hand already reaching for the pistol tucked into his waistband. She watched the motion. The gun was for show; his real weapon was in his size. He was big, but not smart. She made her breathing go erratic, choking and gagging until spit bubbled out her lips. Vernon made the mistake of coming close enough to check her pulse.

She clocked him with the chair leg, full force, right above the knee. He didn't scream —

just gurgled, knees buckling, eyes stunned. She used the momentum to pitch herself and the chair backwards; they hit the floor together in a tangled heap. The zip-tie dug deeper, but her fractured hand slipped out slick with blood and sweat. She landed hard on the point of her shoulder, gritting her teeth against the shriek of pain. Vernon scrambled, one hand clawing for the gun, but Pilar was faster.

She twisted onto her knees and bit down on his thumb as he fumbled for the trigger, biting until she tasted copper and his howl filled the house. He punched her in the face, but it was wild, panicked — almost an accident. She spat the chunk of thumb back at him, planted her good foot, and brought the chair down on his temple with a meaty thwack. He was out before he hit the floor. The babyface kid in the living room stood up, mouth a perfect O, phone sliding from his hand.

Pilar didn't delay. She lunged for Vernon's gun and fired before she had time to think — one round, center mass. The kid went over backwards, limbs thrashing, then lay still. The house, for a second, was dead silent except for the pointless yammer of the TV.

Pilar staggered to her feet, blinking blood

out of her eyelashes, adrenaline buzzing so hard her teeth chattered. She stepped over Vernon's corpse, took the pistol in both hands, and found the third man cowering in the yard behind the screen door, hoping she wouldn't see him. Pilar fired twice—first, the shot tore into the porch post. As he bolted, she squeezed the trigger again. The bullet slammed into his back, sending him crashing forward. Pilar went back inside and found the car keys on Vernon's body, took his wallet for good measure, then fished her own phone out of his back pocket.

She bolted out, barefoot, moving with muscle memory. The van they brought her in was still parked near the back of the compound. She climbed in, slammed the door shut, and threw it into gear. Before she peeled off, she noticed something in the back—a duffel bag half-zipped, slumped against the wall. She yanked it open. Cash. Bundles of it. Blood money.

She hesitated for less than a second, then stuffed as much as she could into her tote bag, tossed a hoodie over herself, and tore off into the night. When she finally felt safe enough to stop, she pulled into a gas station lot and used a burner phone she'd taken off one of the kidnappers. Her fingers trembled as she dialed the only number she trusted.

Genevieve picked up immediately. "Hello."

"It's me, Pilar," she whispered.

"Thank goodness. I was worried sick. Precious devised a plan, but we never heard back from the kidnapper. I feared the worst," Genevieve's voice cracked with emotion.

"I'm sorry. I should have called sooner, but I just kept driving until I felt safe."

"Did they harm you?"

"I'm a bit banged up, but I'm alive. The same can't be said for those men," Pilar replied.

"They're dead?" Genevieve was shocked.

"Yes. I had no other choice. It was them or me," Pilar explained.

"No need to justify. You're alive, and that's all that matters."

"After I escaped, I found some money in the van. I'm keeping it and leaving Houston. I can't handle being in the middle of a war. Not like this."

There was a pause on the line. Genevieve then released a long breath, as if she'd been holding it in.

"That's the wisest decision you've made all year."

"I'll keep in touch," Pilar said, her voice wavering. "I just need some time."

Genevieve didn't protest. "Get out clean. And don't look back."

"I love you, Genevieve, and thank you."

"I love you too."

Pilar ended the call and gazed at the road ahead. No plan, no destination. Just the desire for distance. She merged onto the highway, vanishing into the darkness.

Genevieve knew something was wrong the second she stepped into the garage. The air was too still. Her instincts—trained through trauma, sharpened by survival—screamed at her before logic caught up. She'd just told her driver to take the morning off. She needed space. Needed to breathe. She'd planned to slip into work lowkey, no makeup, no entourage. But the moment she pressed the key fob and heard nothing—no chirp, no blink—her hand instinctively moved to her purse.

The van parked three cars over shouldn't have been there. Black, no plates, front windows down just enough for someone to slide a weapon through. She turned on her heel, heart thudding—but it was too late. Two men emerged, fast and precise.

Genevieve didn't scream. She dropped her bag and pivoted like a sprinter off the blocks, heels cracking concrete. One man lunged, barely missing her shoulder. She spun, grabbed the side mirror of her car, and used it for leverage to slam her elbow into his throat.

The second man reached for a stun gun—she kneed him in the gut and went for his face. But he clipped her jaw with the butt of the taser and she stumbled. That's when the blast hit.

The garage door exploded open, and Precious stormed through in all black—no warning, no finesse—just fire. Dre flanked her with a sawed-off, Midas holding an AR like it was a sacred text, his focus unbreakable.

"GET THE FUCK OFF HER!" Precious voice roared through the streets.

The world narrowed to a tunnel, time stretching and snapping with the rush of adrenaline and the sharp taste of *is-this-it*. Genevieve's hand barely brushed the purse when the air shattered—the first blast from Dre's sawed-off hit the SUV's windshield, ringing out like thunder pounding on a steel drum. Laminated safety glass atomized; the man behind it jerked, mouth opening as his upper chest erupted in a pink mist. The other side of the car, Midas's AR whispered in controlled three-round bursts, popping out the tires, then the doors, then anything that moved behind the sudden spiderweb of broken glass and shrieking metal.

Genevieve ducked, not sure who screamed—maybe her, maybe the car, maybe the city itself. She felt someone's hand on her back, shoving her down, and the pulse of fire as a round ripped past and scalped a chunk of her hair. She could taste blood—her own? Someone else's? It didn't matter. Her body was all animal, moving in a choreography she'd never rehearsed: she crawled, rolled, came up beside the rear wheel, clutching her purse as if it held her whole past life. Over the engine noise and her own heartbeat, she heard Precious's voice: "MOVE!" Then another round of thunder from Dre, precise as a funeral bell.

One of Cortez's men, the one with the gold tooth and the tattooed teardrop, tried to scramble out the passenger side with a submachine gun. He barely got the muzzle up before Midas tagged him in the shoulder, spinning him in place, then Dre finished the job with a gut shot that left him folded over the curb like a broken lawn chair. For a second, it was over. The air settled, thick with cordite, burned oil, and the sudden, shocking silence of bodies not moving.

Genevieve exhaled and tried to stand. Her knees buckled. She put a palm down, smearing blood and gravel on the sidewalk, but she got up. She saw Precious, who hadn't ducked at all, striding forward with the slow-motion calm of someone who'd counted on this exact scenario. Precious yanked open the SUV's back door, found it empty, and spat on the ground in disgust.

Dre checked the fallen men with the practiced tap-tap of a boot to the ribs—one grunted, the other was already gone. Midas reloaded, eyes never leaving the perimeter. Genevieve pulled herself upright, managed to check her reflection in the glass: blood from a surface scalp wound, nothing serious. But her gaze was different now. She didn't look shocked. She looked... elemental. As if fear had burned off, leaving only pure distilled intent.

"You good?" Precious asked, voice crisp.

Genevieve wiped the blood off her cheek with the back of her hand and gave a single nod. "Let's end this. I want all those muthafuckers dead."

Chapter Nineteen

They parked three blocks from the target, dusk only just conceding to night. Dre rode shotgun, face lit by the cold blue of his phone, tapping through two final firewall kills—a digital needle threading through the brick-and-mortar arteries of the East End. Next to him, Midas rechecked the battered duffel in his lap, then cracked the van door. A gust of humid, gasoline-laced air rolled in.

Genevieve stepped onto the sidewalk last, gun drawn but hidden under the lie of a designer trench. Renny moved beside her, calm as a man heading to the post office, not a war. At this hour, no one lingered outside the warehouse— Cortez's men lurked in darkness, unaware Dre had sent his drone ahead, silently cataloging each patrol pattern and security position. Three outside. Five, maybe six, in the main bay. Genevieve made quick eye contact with Precious across the street, a nod as crisp as a bank note.

A siren wailed somewhere distant. Not for them. Not yet. Dre peeled off toward the access ladder, Midas in his wake. Renny and Genevieve threaded through the alley, boots crunching gravel, heartbeats synced. They reached the side entrance just as the lights cut out. Midas's work. The city block went black, and in the pitch, sound took the place of sight: frantic Spanish, the slap of shoes on concrete, the metallic click of safeties coming off.

Genevieve counted to three under her breath. On "two," Renny blew the lock off with a shoebox-sized breacher and kicked the door inward. She led the entry, sweeping left, gun raised. A man lunged from behind a workbench— she shot him in the collarbone, watched him fold. Another guard scurried in the dark, fired wild, then caught a bullet to the cheek from Renny. The first room cleared in eight seconds. Genevieve's shoes were already sticky with blood.

They advanced. In the main bay, the only light came from the emergency glow of an EXIT sign and the burning tip of a cigarette. Cortez was there, surrounded by loyalists, half of whom were already panicking as Dre's drone zipped past the skylight, spraying glass on everyone below.

"Get down!" Genevieve shouted. Two of the men hesitated, unsure if the order was for them. She didn't hesitate—shot one in the thigh, another in the gut. Precious rolled a flashbang through the debris, covering her ears. The world went white, soundless, then full of the shrieks of men who'd suddenly gone blind.

Cortez and two of his men attempted to flee. They almost reached a side corridor when Dre caught up, tackling one of the men from behind and twisting his arms back until his shoulder joints were on the verge of dislocating. Midas quickly moved in to subdue Cortez and the remaining guard, using his full weight to bring all three men crashing to the floor. With a gun pressed to the guard's neck, the struggle intensified until the weapon discharged, killing him.

"On your knees," Genevieve commanded

Cortez as he tried to make another escape attempt. She pressed her pistol firmly against his temple, her hands steady.

Cortez looked up, his lip split and one eye already swelling shut, yet he still managed to smirk. "You think this ends with me? You don't even know what you started."

The room fell silent, except for the rasping breaths of someone dying in the corner. Genevieve locked eyes with Cortez, ready to end him.

"No, Cortez," she said. "You don't," but when she pulled the trigger it jammed giving Cortez an opportunity to reach for a gun near one of his dead guards aiming it at Genevieve.

Right as Cortez was about to pull the trigger, a shot rang out. Not from his weapon, but Renny's. The bullet punched through the back of Cortez's skull, spraying brain and bone onto the concrete. He slumped forward, dead before his knees hit the ground.

Genevieve stared at the body, chest rising and falling, the adrenaline refusing to leave. For a second, she felt nothing—then everything at once, a rush of raw terror, relief and satisfaction.

Precious entered the bay, phone raised, already dialing. "We need to move. Cops are two minutes out."

Renny wiped the muzzle of his gun on Cortez's shirt, then took Genevieve's hand.

"It's done," he murmured, voice low enough for her alone.

Genevieve looked back one last time at the mess they'd made, then followed Renny out, into the bleeding edge of morning. The safehouse in Fifth Ward was already ashes. Renny's crew had torched it after cleaning it out.

The team reassembled in a warehouse off Jensen, red light bouncing off the metal walls. Tensions still high.

"Once again, you saved my life. First, with Arnez and now with Cortez," she said as tears swelled in her eyes. Renny embraced her, holding Genevieve close. It was the first moment since the day had begun that she felt a sense of security, finally at ease in her husband's arms.

"Please tell me, we put an end to this war tonight."

Renny nodded. "The final steps are in motion."

He turned to a screen showing a drone feed—Cortez's last compound in East Downtown, nestled between two fake export companies. Dre leaned over the table. "We hit it in two. No mercy. No survivors."

Genevieve's eyes rested on Precious. "And Shay?"

"Eventually she folded. Told us everything, even bullshit we didn't need to know," Precious winked.

Genevieve inhaled. "And?"

"She's not a problem anymore," Precious assured her.

No one asked if Shay was alive. No one needed to.

The house was quiet. Too quiet. Genevieve moved through the master bedroom barefoot, her robe cinched tight, hair flowing loosely around her shoulders. The storm had passed—or so she thought. Cortez was dead. Shay was handled. Pilar was safe. And for the first time in weeks, she could feel herself exhale.

Renny stood at the edge of the terrace, shirtless, its marble tiles gleaming under the soft glow of the moonlight. The air was rich with the scent of jasmine from the meticulously manicured garden below. In one hand, he cradled a glass of D'USSÉ, the amber liquid catching the light like liquid gold, while his other hand gripped the ornate iron railing, intricately designed with swirling patterns that spoke of craftsmanship and luxury. He leaned slightly forward, as if challenging the night to come for them again. In the distance, the Houston skyline shimmered softly with a golden hue, the city was finally at peace.

Genevieve slid in behind her husband, arms around his waist, head on his back. "It's over," she whispered.

Renny didn't answer. He just nodded, slow, believing it to be over and he could breathe. Then Genevieve's phone buzzed on the nightstand. Not a call. Not a number she knew, just a video. She walked over, frowned, thumbed the screen. And then she saw it.

The image jolted to life—grainy, flickering, but unmistakable. Amir. Her nephew. Genesis's son. Blood caked to his temple, a gag shoved in his mouth, arms bound behind his back in some desolate cage. A voice offscreen—low, taunting, familiar—said, ***Smile for the camera, little prince.***

The phone slipped from her hand and hit the hardwood with a brutal crack. Genevieve collapsed to her knees.

"NO—" she gasped, one hand to her mouth,

the other clawing at the floor, trying to rewind, to unsee it.

Renny was there in seconds, grabbing the phone, watching it with widening eyes. He didn't speak. Didn't curse. Just stared.

And then he turned, his voice hoarse, full of fury he couldn't even shape into words.

"They got Amir," Genevieve whispered, trembling.

Renny's jaw clenched. "That muthfucka couldn't get you... so he took Genesis's son."

Genevieve wiped her face with a shaking hand. "They want to break us. All of us."

Renny set the phone down gently. And walked out the room.

Not fast. Not panicked. But with the kind of rage that moves like thunder—slow, building, inevitable. Downstairs, the war wasn't over. It was just about to begin again.

Epilogue...

Two weeks later outside the Greyhound terminal. Downtown Houston. Pilar stepped off the bus like a ghost walking back into the fire. Hair pulled low beneath a hoodie, oversized sunglasses shielding swollen eyes, jeans baggy and bunched over scuffed sneakers. The duffel slung across her shoulder wasn't designer—it was military-grade, the kind used by men who don't return home. Inside it? Cash. A burner phone. A loaded Glock. She moved like someone who'd seen the edge—and jumped anyway.

The terminal buzzed with the usual: kids crying, old heads mumbling to themselves, girls fresh out the system dragging plastic bags full of folded dreams. But Pilar didn't hear any of it. She had tunnel vision. One mission. One name. Brice. He thought she was gone. Thought she ran. That's what she let him believe. The truth? She sat in a cheap motel for days, gun in her lap, phone off, hands shaking from everything she'd lost and everything she was ready to take back.

Now she was back in the city—dead in the eyes, but sharper than ever.

Pilar caught a ride across town, paid cash, didn't speak. Told the driver to drop her two blocks from Brice's place. Just in case.

The condo building hadn't changed. Still slick, still sitting like a throne in the middle of Uptown. But the doorman? Gone. The lights in the lobby? Dimmer than she remembered. Even the flowers outside were wilted. Maybe an omen the empire was crumbling.

She slipped past the side gate, made her way to the stairwell—took the steps two at a time. Her heartbeat didn't spike until she reached the door. His door. 3B. She knocked once. Silence. Then—footsteps. Light. Familiar. He cracked the door just enough to peek. "Yo—?"

She raised the Glock. Brice's eyes went wide. Too late. POP.

One shot to the chest. Then another. She watched him stumble back, hand clutched to his shirt, shock smeared across his face. He dropped. Pilar stepped over the threshold, aimed again, but something in her paused. Not mercy. Just exhaustion. She stood there for a moment, chest heaving, the apartment stretching out behind him like a broken promise. She looked down at the man she'd once trusted, wanted, almost loved.

"You played the wrong bitch," she whispered.

Then she turned, stepped back into the hallway, and walked out without looking back. Hours later a security camera caught her boarding the next outbound bus. Hair still tucked. Sunglasses still on. No luggage. No name. She took a window seat in the back. Didn't cry, as she had no regrets. Just stared out into the night as the city disappeared behind her. Where was she going? Even she didn't know. But she had the money. And soon—she'd have a new life. The next chapter was already calling. Somewhere across the Gulf, a yacht waited.

TO BE CONTINUED IN: YACHT GIRL –
The Perfect Companion

Coming Soon

A KING PRODUCTION

Yacht Girl

Behind every
yacht, is a secret...

A Novelette

JOY DEJA KING

A Titillating Tale

Mastermind...

A Novelette

JOY DEJA KING

Chapter One

"Mr. Richardson, please come with me," the doctor said, gesturing for Cartier to follow him and a nurse into a room at the hospital.

"How is my wife? Is she getting better?" Cartier asked, concern in his voice as the nurse shut the door behind them.

"I'm afraid I have some unfortunate news to share. Despite our best efforts, Lila has passed away," the doctor informed Cartier somberly.

"I'm sorry doctor, why are we here... where

is my wife?" Cartier demanded, in denial, refusing to believe a word the doctor said.

"Sir, my name is Cynthia Johnson," the nurse spoke up, introducing herself formally. "I've been treating your wife during her recent visits. I can take you to see her, but Lila is no longer with us," she said gently, placing a comforting hand on Cartier's shoulder. "We know this isn't easy, and we're here to support you in any way we can."

"I'm sorry, Mr. Richardson, but I have another patient I need to attend to," the doctor explained. "But if you need anything, Cynthia is available to assist you," he added before leaving.

Cynthia sat down next to Cartier and asked, "Is there anything I can get for you? Would you like to see your wife?"

"I don't want to see Lila likc that. I want to remember my wife for the beautiful, vibrant woman that she was. Not..." his voice cracked and trailed off.

"I completely understand," Cynthia said sympathetically. "But I do need you to sign some papers so we can release her personal belongings to you." She handed him a pen and the documents from a manilla envelope.

As Cartier signed the papers, he felt the weight of reality sink in. He remained sitting in the empty room, his face buried in his hands. Cynthia tried to offer comfort, but there was nothing she could do to ease his pain. As a nurse, she had delivered news of loved ones' deaths many times before, but it never got any easier. She always took a deep breath before entering a room, knowing that what she was about to say would change someone's life forever.

Cartier looked up with a distant gaze in his eyes. "What am I going to do without my wife? She's the love of my life." He paused and then corrected himself. "She was the love of my life." He swallowed hard, finally accepting that Lila was no longer with him.

Six Months Later...

"Cartier, our clients will be here in fifteen minutes. Do you want to have the meeting in your office or the conference room?" Callie, his Senior Marketing Executive, asked.

"Let's use the conference room. Please make sure Audra has everything set up and ready. I don't want any delays," he said while reading through some key points he wanted to address during the meeting.

"Actually, Audra is currently training a temp that was sent over to cover for Rachel."

"The receptionist... What happened to her?"

"No idea. Audra mentioned that Rachel called early this morning, saying there was a family emergency, and she needed a few weeks off. Audra's busy with the temp, so I'll have Donovan double check to ensure everything is prepared."

"Just get it done," Cartier said dismissively without looking up from his work. "And close my door."

Callie let out a frustrated sigh as she left Cartier's office. "Audra, can you please wrap up this training and meet me in the conference room? I have more important tasks for you to do." She snapped.

"Of course, Callie. Just give me one moment." Audra gave a polite smile before rolling her eyes once Callie was out of sight. "That woman is so annoying. Just because she's fuckin' the boss, she thinks she's the queen bee."

"Wow, I wasn't expecting that tea to be spilled," Serenity chimed in as she settled into her seat at the receptionist desk. "Especially since I'm only here through a temporary employment agency, so technically I don't even work here."

"That's true, which makes it even easier for me to freely run my mouth," Audra laughed. "Sorry not sorry, but Callie is truly a piece of work. The moment Mr. Richardson's wife died she pounced on him like a dog in heat. And mind you, he was screwing two other women who worked here. Both of them ended up getting fired because Callie thought eliminating the competition would increase her chances of becoming the next Cartier Richardson."

"How long ago did his wife pass away?"

"Lila passed away about six months ago. She was so young; it was unexpected and heartbreaking."

"And he's already involved with three different women?" Serenity asked in shock.

"Yes, and three is all that worked in this office. Mr. Richardson has quite the reputation as a ladies' man. Some say his behavior escalated after his wife passed away as a way to cope with his grief. Others claim he always had multiple women in rotation but was more discreet when his wife was alive."

"Interesting. Well, I'm just here to do my job and stay out of any drama," Serenity replied, eager to start working. "I need the paycheck, not the gossip."

"Girl, I feel you, but I need the paycheck. drama and the gossip," Audra laughed. "Working here is like being in a real-life soap opera, and I love it," she grinned before noticing her boss and his right-hand man walking towards them. "Good morning, Mr. Richardson and Mr. Upton!"

Both men responded dryly with a simple "good morning."

"Do you know where Callie is?" asked Cartier, looking slightly vexed.

"Yes, she's in the conference room," Audra replied, her smile never faltering as she maintained her professional demeanor.

"Thank you," said Cartier, hurrying off in the direction of the conference room.

"If you're not in the know, that's our CEO, Cartier Richardson. And the distinguished gentleman walking with him is Bradley Upton, a key player in our company's success. Some say he's really the brains and moral center behind it all, but his loyalty to Cartier never wavers," explained Audra to Serenity.

Serenity found herself completely focused on Bradley Upton. She was curious about his connection to Cartier for various reasons but kept her thoughts to herself in front of Audra. Instead, she directed her comments towards Cartier specifically.

"Mr. Richardson certainly looks the part. That suit he's wearing must have cost a grip," Serenity observed, taking note of the flawlessly tailored Kiton two-piece suit in tonal plaid, with its sharp notched lapels and white-stitched cotton pocket square. The overall look was effortlessly stylish, thanks to a casual navy Kiton cashmere-blend crew-neck t-shirt worn underneath. Dripping with a few brilliant cut diamonds, Cartier definitely knew how to flaunt his wealth.

"Oh yeah," Audra agreed. "Mr. Richardson plays no games when it comes to fashion. He only wants the best." She paused, realizing they needed to finish their conversation later. "But I better get going to the conference room before I get in trouble for gossiping too much. I'll check in on you later though. You have my cell number if you need anything," she said with a wink before rushing off.

As Serenity tried to process everything, she had learned that morning about Cartier Richardson and Bradley Upton, her phone began ringing non-stop.

"Looks like it's going to be a busy day," she said, feeling a mix of nervousness and excitement about what awaited her at her new job.

A KING PRODUCTION

Baller Bitches

VOLUME 1
PARTS 1-3

A NOVEL

JOY DEJA KING

Diamond

"Bitch, you ain't shit!" When my baby daddy stood in front of me screaming that bullshit with spit flying everywhere, I kept putting the clear coat of polish on my nails ignoring his ass. "Did you hear what the fuck I said?" he belted as the vein in the middle of his forehead started pulsating.

"Mutherfucka, everybody in the damn building can hear what the fuck you just said. Are you done ranting 'cause I got shit to do?"

"That's what's wrong wit yo' ass, yo' mouth too fuckin' slick."

"Umm this shit gettin' repetitive. Ain't but so many ways you can call me a bitch and tell me I ain't shit. I get it, you think I'm foul. So either come up with some new descriptions or move on to something else."

"I can't believe I got a baby wit' yo' stupid ass. You don't give a fuck about nobody but yourself. One day I promise I'ma take our daughter away from you because I refuse to let her grow up and end up like you."

I put my polish down and eyeballed Rico because I wanted him to know what I was about to say wasn't a game. "Nigga, the day you start plotting to take my daughter away from me is the day you better tell yo' mama to start making your funeral arrangements. You can call me every ho, dick sucker, no good bitch all mutherfuckin' day but when you bring Destiny into the mix we have a problem. Now please get the fuck out my crib and take that noise you spewing someplace else."

"Diamond, this shit ain't over. I'll be back tomorrow to pick up my daughter for the weekend and she better be here and not at your mother's house."

"I tell you what. Why don't you pick Destiny up from my mother's house tomorrow because I can't take having to see yo' ass two days in a row."

"No, I'll pick Destiny up from here tomorrow. So whatever partying and fucking you planning on doing tonight make sure you have yo' ass up in time to get my daughter in the morning."

"That's what your problem is now. So busy worrying about what the fuck I'm doing," I huffed under my breath not wanting to reignite the argument because I was ready for Rico to bounce.

"Bye," I said keeping my head down, until I heard the door shut.

There was a time an argument with Rico would fuck up my entire day but this shit had become so routine I barely broke a sweat over it now. See, there was a time when Rico was actually my boyfriend. I thought we would be together forever but that was when I was young and dumb. He swooped me up when I was fifteen and not used to good dick or money. When I was walking home from school one afternoon he pulled up in a tricked out Benz and I couldn't believe when he rolled down the window asking me for my name. He was one of those pretty niggas who knew his packaging was right.

From that day on we started dating. Rico would pick me up from school almost everyday and them chick's mouths dropped every time he pulled up and I would get in the car. We would go get something to eat and just talked. Although he was three years older than me he never made me feel like a kid instead I felt like a woman. But I wasn't a woman and Rico was way out of my league. He quickly made me his girl but that didn't keep him from having mad other bitches, so many I couldn't keep count. In the beginning I fell for all his lies. He had a valid excuse for every accusation I had. By the time I woke up to the truth it was two years later and I was pregnant with Destiny.

That was the roughest nine months of my life.

I had bitches calling my phone harassing me. They would say my man just left their crib and he fucked the shit out of them. My feet swelled up, belly poked out feeling depressed and helpless having to hear this shit. By this time, Rico wasn't even trying to hide his dirt anymore. He felt I was pregnant and stuck. Even after all that I stayed with Rico. It took another year before I wised up and gave that nigga the deuces. When I did, Rico tried to make my life a living hell. I guess he thought I would be a dumbass forever...not!

I spent the first year of Destiny's life being with her day and night while Rico ran the streets. I don't even remember him changing one diaper. But I loved her so much it didn't even matter. Destiny was like my real life baby doll and she helped me get my shit together. I had gained so much weight during my pregnancy and even more afterwards and I think it was out of depression, because Rico had me so stressed out. I decided I had to get myself back on point and I started taking Destiny out in her stroller everyday. Within six months I had walked all that weight off. After that you couldn't tell me nothing, including Rico. I went from being a sad, miserable bitch to a baller bitch.

P.O. Box 912
Collierville, TN 38027

www.joydejaking.com
@preciouscummingsofficial

ORDER FORM

Name:

Address:

City/State:

Zip:

QUANTITY	TITLES	PRICE	TOTAL
	Bitch	$17.99	
	Bitch Reloaded	$17.99	
	The Bitch Is Back	$17.99	
	Queen Bitch	$17.99	
	Last Bitch Standing	$17.99	
	Superstar	$17.99	
	Ride Wit' Me	$17.99	
	Ride Wit' Me Part 2	$17.99	
	Stackin' Paper	$17.99	
	Trife Life To Lavish	$17.99	
	Trife Life To Lavish II	$17.99	
	Stackin' Paper II	$17.99	
	Rich or Famous	$17.99	
	Rich or Famous Part 2	$17.99	
	Rich or Famous Part 3	$17.99	
	Bitch A New Beginning	$17.99	
	Mafia Princess Part 1	$17.99	
	Mafia Princess Part 2	$17.99	
	Mafia Princess Part 3	$17.99	
	Mafia Princess Part 4	$17.99	
	Mafia Princess Part 5	$17.99	
	Boss Bitch	$17.99	
	Baller Bitches Vol. 1	$17.99	
	Baller Bitches Vol. 2	$17.99	
	Baller Bitches Vol. 3	$17.99	
	Bad Bitch	$17.99	
	Still The Baddest Bitch	$17.99	
	Power	$17.99	
	Power Part 2	$17.99	
	Drake	$17.99	
	Drake Part 2	$17.99	
	Female Hustler	$17.99	
	Female Hustler Part 2	$17.99	

QUANTITY	TITLES	PRICE	TOTAL
	Female Hustler Part 3	$17.99	
	Female Hustler Part 4	$17.99	
	Female Hustler Part 5	$17.99	
	Female Hustler Part 6	$17.99	
	Princess Fever "Birthday Bash"	$6.00	
	Nico Carter The Men Of The Bitch Series	$17.99	
	Bitch The Beginning Of The End	$17.99	
	Supreme...Men Of The Bitch Series	$17.99	
	Bitch The Final Chapter	$17.99	
	Stackin' Paper III	$17.99	
	Men Of The Bitch Series And The Women Who Love Them	$17.99	
	Coke Like The 80s	$17.99	
	Baller Bitches The Reunion Vol. 4	$17.99	
	Stackin' Paper IV	$17.99	
	The Legacy	$17.99	
	Lovin' Thy Enemy	$17.99	
	Stackin' Paper V	$17.99	
	The Legacy Part 2	$17.99	
	Assassins - Episode 1	$12.99	
	Assassins - Episode 2	$12.99	
	Assassins - Episode 3	$12.99	
	Bitch Chronicles	$40.00	
	So Hood So Rich	$17.99	
	Stackin' Paper VI	$17.99	
	Female Hustler Part 7	$17.99	
	Toxic...	$12.99	
	Stackin' Paper VII	$17.99	
	Sugar Babies...	$12.99	
	Deadly Divorce...	$12.99	
	The Legacy Part 3	$17.99	
	BITCH The Story of Precious Cummings	$17.99	
	Mastermind...	$12.99	
	Stackin' Paper VIII	$17.99	
	Stackin' Paper Holiday	$12.99	
	Mastermind 2...	$12.99	
	Baller Bitches Vol. 5	$17.99	
	Mastermind 3...	$12.99	
	Trife Life To Lavish III	$17.99	

Shipping/Handling (Via Priority Mail) $11.00 1-3 Books, $19.99 4-10 Books. For 11 or more $24.75.
Total: $__________FORMS OF ACCEPTED PAYMENTS: Certified or government issued checks and
money Orders, all mail in orders take 5-7 Business days to be delivered